哈福

哈福

哈福

Fast

說英語，像開自來水

大膽說！
流利英語的捷徑

張瑪麗◎著

放膽說，不怕錯，
你的英語就成功了！

哈福

史上最簡單的英語會話
說英語，像開自來水

在講究提升自我競爭「優勢」的時代中，學習英語是增加自我價值不可缺少的一環。然而很多人都有同樣的經驗：為了英語，花了不少錢，用了不少時間，卻還是開不了口說幾句英語。

為解決學習者這個困擾，以及符合社會重視效率的快速學習速度，讓你在最短的時間內，學會最重要、每天都用得上的40句話，很快就可以掌握英語表達技巧。

每一Unit中，老師會詳細解說每一句英語的用法、使用場合，還介紹和這個用句相類似或相關的語句字詞，使讀者對它的用法有更深入的了解。會話部分，生動的短句可提高讀者對學習英語的樂趣，因樂趣而容易持續學習，將過去沒學好的，一次補回來！

翻開這本書，讀者一定會發現書裡的英文單字都很簡單，幾乎不用再花時間去背，且應用的範圍很廣泛；書中也沒有艱澀的文法，只要你一課一課看下去，很自然地學一項用一項，很快地，你就能融會貫通，舉一反三，開口說英語。

擁有最好的學習工具，學習才能事半功倍，學英語當然也就變得輕而易舉！讀者只要配合我們所精心製作的MP3，不斷反覆練習，假以時日，就可以學會這些最自然得體的措詞，以及英美人士的說話方式，在適當的情境下說出適當的英語。

「讓英語存在我的腦海中，要用時如自來水般的自然流出來，不亦樂乎！」現在就準備好你的眼、口和耳，跨出流利英語的第一步！

一般人學習英語十幾年，還不會應用，不敢開口，本書讓您重建信心，把英語說得和母語一樣好，語言生動活潑，在短期內發揮十足潛力，一舉成功。

如此一來，無論考試、求職、晉升或與老外聊天，您都可以行遍天下無敵手，溝通無國界。

聰明學英文，So Easy！

你還記得你怎麼學中文的嗎？在你會看中文之前，在你會寫中文之前，在你還很小的時候，你周遭的人在講話，你就跟著說，你絕不會在乎你說的對不對，好像你每講一個字，一句話，身旁的大人都覺得很不可思議，你就越講越高興，我們就用同樣的方法來學英語吧。所以，大膽講、勇敢說，不要怕說錯；不管你怎麼說，老外都聽得懂。

我們美國公司所製作的每一本英語學習書，都是模擬美國人每天說的話，你在我們所製作的英語書裡，所學到每一句英語，都可以隨時用來跟美國人說，美國人一定聽得懂，每一句話保證都是純美語，我們要你天天聽，時時聽，有空就聽，聽了之後，你就得跟著說，那如果聽不懂，怎麼跟著說呢？

所以，我們錄製MP3時，都會有先用慢慢的速度念，我們要求美籍老師慢慢唸的原因就是，要讓你先聽得懂，這樣你才能夠跟著說。

快速說英文，So Quickly！

你看電視或是看電影的時候，會不會覺得美國人說英語說的很快，好像每一個字都是連成一個字說出來的，實際上，美國人還是一字一字分開說的，只是語調的關係，所以聽起來，好像一句話裡的每個字都是連成一個字。

我們的MP3先以慢的速度念給你聽，目的在讓你聽得懂，可以跟著唸，等你會跟著唸之後，你還要學會聽懂美國人說英語的正常語調，你如果能夠聽熟他們的語調，你會發現，他們說的英語其實也是一個字一個字的說的。當你聽得懂美國老師以正常速度念英語時，你就是英語達人了。

CONTENTS

Part 2 用最簡單的英語和外國人做生意 193

Part 1

用最簡單的英語
和外國人聊不停

1. No kidding!
你不是在開玩笑吧！

No Kidding! That's great!

文法句型解說

No kidding!

kid這個字在口語的說法，可以做「開玩笑」的意思，片語 No kidding! 可以用來表示你有點驚訝對方說的話，或你不完全相信對方說的話，所以當對方告訴你一件事，令你有點吃驚時，你就可以回答他說 No kidding!，意思是說「真的？你不是在開玩笑吧？」遇到這種情形，你除了說 No kidding! 之外，也可以說 You are not kidding me, are you?

No kidding!

No kidding! 這個片語用在當對方告訴你一件事，而這件事大家都已經知道了，你說 No kidding! 含有「你才

知道啊！」或是你帶有點同意的語氣說「可不是嘛！」
例如：這幾天天氣很熱，你的朋友走過來跟你說，這幾
天實在很熱，你可以回答他說 No kidding!，這裡的 No
kidding! 就含有「可不是嘛！」的意思。

說得漂亮--實況會話

●當聽到有人升遷時，這樣回答就會很動聽。

W I got promoted to vice president.

M *No kidding!* That's great!

W 我高升做副總裁。
M 真的，那很棒。

Tip !---英語小知識

be promoted to

promote 這個字是當動詞，意思是「晉升到高階一點、
責任較重的職位」，如果某人是被動升到某一個較高的
職位，那英語的說法就要用「被動式（be promoted to
某一個較高的職位）」。

●贊同別人的說法時，你可以這樣說。

W It looks like I'm putting on a little
weight.

M *No kidding!*

W 我看起來好像胖了一點。
M 可不是嘛！

put on weight

put on weight 是個片語，就是「胖了」的意思。

lose weight

lose weight 這個片語，與上一個片語意思相反，就是「瘦了」的意思，也可以説「減肥」。

● 有同感時，也可以這樣說。

[W] It sure is hot and humid.

[M] *No kidding!*

[W] 今天真的又熱又悶。
[M] 就是説嘛！

快熟句型---記住真好用

- Mary's 49 years old? No kidding!
  瑪麗四十九歲了？你不是在開玩笑吧？

- You are not kidding me, are you?
  你不是在開玩笑吧？

- I've been putting on some weight lately.
  我最近胖了一些。

  I think I have to go on a diet
  我想我得節食才行。

● I feel so good today.
我今天心情好得很。

I've been trying to diet and it hasn't been easy, but I have lost weight.
我一直在節食，那挺不容易的，但體重是減輕了。

Tip !---英語小知識

diet

diet 這個字當名詞，就是指「為了某種疾病，醫生特別指定的飲食」，或是「減肥用的特殊飲食」。diet 這個字當動詞，就是「節食」或是「按照醫生規定的食物進食」的意思。

超實用單字---1秒就記住

kid [kɪd]	（動）戲弄；欺騙；開玩笑
promote [prə'mot]	（動）晉升；擢升
vice [vaɪs]	（形）副的
president ['prɛzədənt]	（名）總裁
weight [wet]	（名）重量
humid ['hjumɪd]	（形）潮濕的
diet ['daɪət]	（形）（飲料）低糖的 （動）節食 （名）（減肥或治病用的）特殊飲食
lately ['letlɪ]	（副）近來；最近
on a diet	節食

2. I was only kidding.
我只是在開玩笑。

I was only kidding.

文法句型解說

I was only kidding.

當你說了一句話，然後又要告訴對方，你只是在開玩
笑，英語的說法就是 I was only kidding. 或 I was
just kidding.

You've got to be kidding!

當你幾乎不相信對方所說的話時，你可以跟對方說，
「你一定是在開玩笑」，表示你不相信他說的話，你認
為他是在開玩笑，英語的說法就是 You've got to be
kidding! 或 You're kidding! 或 You're kidding me!

I'm not kidding.

在上一單元我們說過，kid 可以當「開玩笑」的意思，所以你若是要告訴對方，「我不是在開玩笑，我說的是真的」，英語的說法就是 I am not kidding. 你也可以說 I kid you not. 或把主詞「I」省略掉，直接說 Kid you not.

說得漂亮--實況會話

● 在嚇唬到別人後，要表達只是開玩笑，可以這樣說。

M You look like you're putting on some weight, Mary.

W Really! Oh no!

It must have been that ice cream Sundae I had yesterday.

M Mary, you're overreacting.

I was only kidding.

W Don't scare me like that, John.

M 瑪麗，你看起來好像胖了。

W 真的，糟糕。
一定是我昨天吃的冰淇淋聖代。

M 瑪麗，你反應過度了。
我只是在開玩笑啊。

W 約翰，別那樣子嚇我。

W Hey Mark, have you seen John around?

M Didn't you hear?

He's under arrest for allegedly embezzling funds from the company.

W Is that right?

He seemed like such an honest person.

M *I kid you not.*

I heard it straight from the top.

W 嘿，馬克，你有沒有看到約翰？

M 你沒有聽説嗎？

他因為被指挪用公款已經被逮捕了。

W 真的？

他人看起來蠻誠實的嘛。

M 我沒有騙你。

我是從公司高層那裡聽來的。

快熟句型---記住真好用

- **Don't** get mad. I was only kidding.

別生氣，我只是在開玩笑。

Tip !---英語小知識

get mad

説到生氣，大家學過的是 angry 這個字，但是英語會話中，説到生氣，經常用 mad 這個字。如果我們説某

個人在生氣，英語的説法就是 He is mad.，但是如果要叫對方別生氣，英語的説法是 Don't get mad.

- **I was just kidding.**
  我只是在開玩笑。

- **You've got to be kidding!**
  你一定是在開玩笑。

- **You're kidding.**
  你在開玩笑。

- **You won the lottery? You're kidding me.**
  你中了彩券？你一定在騙我。

- **Who do you think you're kidding?**
  你想騙誰啊？

- **You wouldn't be trying to kid me, would you?**
  你不會是想騙我的吧？

- **I am not kidding.**
  我可不是在開玩笑。

- **I kid you not.**
  我沒有騙你。

overreact [ˈovəˌrɪˈækt]	（動）反應過度
scare [skɛr]	（動）使害怕
arrest [əˈrɛst]	（名）逮捕
allegedly [əˈlɛdʒɪdlɪ]	（副）（不論真偽）據稱地
embezzle [ɪmˈbɛzḷ]	（動）挪用公款；盜用公款
fund [fʌnd]	（名）基金
company [ˈkʌmpənɪ]	（名）公司
straight [stret]	（形）直接的
top [tɑp]	（名）高職位者；高層人員
won [wʌn]	（動）贏（win的過去式）
lottery [ˈlɑtərɪ]	（名）彩券；六合彩
mad [mæd]	（形）生氣的

Quit pulling my leg.

文法句型解說

Quit pulling my leg.

pull my leg 是個片語，意思是「欺騙我」，或「開我的玩笑」，所以如果你知道對方說的話不是真的，是在騙你的，或是在開玩笑的，你叫他別騙你了，就可以用 quit 這個動詞，quit 的意思是「停止」，在 quit 的後面接動名詞（動詞 + ing），表示叫對方「停止做某件事」，所以你要叫對方別騙你，就是把 pull my leg這個片語改成 pulling my leg，放在 quit 的後面，整句話英語的說法就是 Quit pulling my leg.

Don't pull my leg.

要叫對方別騙你，也可以用命令句的句型。「Don't + 原

形動詞」，是叫對方「不要做某件事」，所以要叫對方別騙你，英語的說法就是 Don't pull my leg.

●要別人不要騙你，這樣說很有趣。

[W] John, what do you think about what Professor Brown is doing to our papers?

[M] I've been sick, so I haven't been in class. What happened?

[W] He's increasing the minimum length to 10 pages.

And he's moving the due date up to next Monday.

[M] *Quit pulling my leg.*

That's too cruel for any professor.

[W] 約翰，布朗教授對我們報告的要求，你認為怎麼樣？

[M] 我病了一陣子，所以一直沒有來上課。
怎麼啦？

[W] 他要求報告最少要十頁。
而且把繳交的日期提前到下星期一。

[M] 不要騙我了。
任何一個教授這麼做，都是太殘忍了。

● Quit pulling my leg. I'm not falling for that.
別騙我了。我不會上當的。

Tip !---英語小知識

I'm not falling for that.

「fall for 某樣東西」，這個片語的意思就是「被某件東西所騙」，所以，你若是要說 「那騙不到我」，或是 「我不會被騙的」，英語的說法就是 I'm not falling for that.

● Don't pull my leg.
別騙我。

● I can't believe you fell for John's story.
我真不相信，你被約翰編造出來的故事騙了。

● Don't believe him. He's just pulling your leg.
不要相信他，他是在騙你的。

● Let me know if he is pulling my leg.
如果他在騙我，跟我說一聲。

● You don't mean that. You're just pulling my leg.
你不是說真心話，你只是在騙我。

quit [kwɪt]	（動）停止
pull [pʊl]	（動）拉
paper [ˈpepɚ]	（名）研究報告
sick [sɪk]	（形）生病的；不舒服的
happen [ˈhæpən]	（動）發生
increase [ɪnˈkris]	（動）增加
minimum [ˈmɪnɪməm]	（形）最低的
length [lɛŋθ]	（名）長度
due [dju]	（形）截止期限的
date [det]	（動）日期
cruel [ˈkruəl]	（形）殘忍的

4. I'm sorry to hear that.
聽到這件事，我很難過。

MP3-5

Oh, I'm so sorry to hear that.

文法句型解說

sorry 表示「難過」

當你聽到某人生病，或是遭遇到什麼不幸的事情，你感到很難過，你就可以跟對方說，I'm sorry to hear that.，表示你覺得很難過。

sorry 表示「遺憾」或是「失望」

當你對某種情況，感到「遺憾、失望」，或是對你所做的事情感到「後悔」或「抱歉」時，就可以說 sorry 來表達，例如：你聽到某人離職了，你感到很遺憾，你就可以說 I'm sorry he's gone.，或是你的朋友去參加宴會回來，你問他玩得愉快嗎，他說不好玩，你就可以說 I'm sorry you didn't have fun. 來表達你的遺憾。

sorry 表示「道歉」

當你做了某件事，引起別人不高興，或是為別人惹來麻煩時，你要跟對方道歉，英語就是跟對方說「sorry」或「I'm sorry.」，來表示「對不起」或「道歉」，例如：大夥兒約好要出去吃飯，但是你正好有電話來，於是大家就等你一個人，所以當你電話結束出來時，你趕緊跟大家抱歉，拖了那麼久，害大家久等，英語的說法就是：

Sorry I took so long.
抱歉，我拖了那麼久。

又例如：約翰打了他的妹妹，妹妹哭了，媽媽就跟約翰說，「去跟你妹妹道歉」，這句話英語的說法就是：

Go say you are sorry to your sister for hitting her, John.

說得漂亮--實況會話

● 深感同情或表示抱歉時，這樣說最有禮貌。

M　What's wrong?
　　You look like you haven't slept in a week.

W　My husband has been diagnosed with cancer.

M　Oh, I'm sorry to hear that.

　　M 怎麼啦？
　　　你看起來好像一個星期沒睡覺了。

Ⓦ 我先生被診斷出患了癌症。

Ⓜ 噢，聽到這個消息，我很難過。

●聽到不好的消息時，可以這樣說。

Ⓜ How did swim team tryouts turn out?

Ⓦ Mary got the last spot on the team.

I'll have to wait till next year.

Ⓜ I'm sorry.

I know how much you really wanted to be a part of the team.

Ⓦ 游泳隊的選拔結果如何？

Ⓜ 瑪麗得到游泳隊最後一個名額。
我必須等明年。

Ⓦ 那真遺憾。
我知道你有多想進入游泳隊。

快熟句型---記住真好用

● I am sorry that you are sick.
聽到你生病，我很難過。

● She was sorry to hear that John had been sick.
她對於約翰一直在生病，感到難過。

● I'm sorry about what's happened.
對所發生的事，我感到遺憾。

- She was very sorry about all the trouble she had caused.

  她對她所造成的麻煩，感到抱歉。

- We are sorry about all the mess.

  弄得亂七八糟的，很對不起。

Tip !---英語小知識

> **mess**
>
> 如果我們說，某個地方真是 a mess，意思就是說「那個地方亂七八糟的，東西丟得滿地」。所以當你回家看到滿屋子亂七八糟時，你就可以大叫一聲，Clean up this mess. 把這亂七八糟的清理乾淨。

- I'm sorry to call so late.

  對不起，這麼晚打電話來。

- Go say you are sorry to your sister for hitting her, John.

  約翰，去跟你妹妹說，你為了打她的事跟她道歉。

超實用單字---1秒就記住

slept [slɛpt]	（動）睡（sleep的過去式）
diagnosed [ˌdaɪəɡˈnost]	（動）被診斷出（diagnose的過去分詞）
cancer [ˈkænsɚ]	（名）癌；癌症
tryout [ˈtraɪˌaʊt]	（名）選拔

spot [spɑt]	（名）位置
team [tim]	（名）隊伍；團隊
last [læst]	（形）最後的
part [pɑrt]	（名）部分
trouble [ˈtrʌbl̩]	（名）麻煩；困難
cause [kɔz]	（動）引起
mess [mɛs]	（名）亂七八糟；一團糟
hit [hɪt]	（名）撞；打

5. Excuse me.
對不起。

Excuse me?

文法句型解說

Excuse me. 表示「打聲招呼」

當你想問對方問題，如果直截了當地問，好像有點不禮貌，所以通常應該先說 Excuse me. 再提出你要問的問題。說Excuse me. 這句話有兩種意義：第一，讓對方注意到你要跟他說話；第二，說 Excuse me 不是在道歉，而是禮貌 地說聲「打擾了，請問一下」，如：

Excuse me, can you tell me the way to the library please?

打擾一下，可否請你告訴我，到圖書館的路怎麼走？

或是你想跟對方搭訕，隨便開個話頭大家好聊聊天，這時你就可以先說聲 Excuse me. 讓對方注意到你要跟他說話，免得你開始說話時，對方並不知道你要跟他說話，而變成你對著空氣說話，等對方發現你是在跟他說

話時，你們兩個人可能都會覺得很尷尬，那可是掃興得很。

Excuse me. 表示「道歉」

Excuse me. 在上一個說法裡並不是在向對方道歉，但是如果你做了什麼事，你覺得這件事有點不禮貌，或是不小心犯了什麼錯，真正要向對方道歉時，也可以說 Excuse me. 來向對方表示歉意。

例如：你不小心撞到對方，或是不小心倒翻了茶水，潑到對方，你就可以趕緊說聲 Excuse me.

又例如：大家一起在吃飯，你打了個嗝，打嗝雖然不是你的錯，但是趕緊說聲 Excuse me.，可是最基本的用餐禮貌。

或是你打了個噴嚏，最好也說聲 Excuse me.

Excuse me. 表示「請讓路」

Excuse me. 也有「請讓路」的意思。有時在較擁擠的場合裡，如果你要請對方讓路，你就可以說 Excuse me.，或者當別人向你說 Excuse me.，希望你讓個路讓他過去時，可千萬別無動於衷地站著一動也不動。

Excuse me. 表示「要告退」

當一夥人在一起，而你要先告退，或是要先離開一下時，說聲 Excuse me.，大家就知道你要先行離開。

Excuse me? 表示「對不起，你說什麼，我沒聽清楚？」

當你沒聽清楚對方說的話，想請對方再重說一遍時，你可以跟他說 Excuse me? 。注意：在這種情形下，說 Excuse me? 時句尾要拉高。

Excuse me? 表示「嘿，你不要亂講！」

當對方說了一句話，或說了一件事情，而你覺得對方的說法不禮貌，或是你覺得對方說的話，你不同意，你覺得對方在亂講時，你都可以說句 Excuse me? 表示「嘿，你不要開玩笑」，或「嘿，你不要亂講」。

有時，對方說的話是在開你玩笑，而你也知道對方是在開你玩笑，你還是得抗議一聲，這種情形，你也是要說 Excuse me? 表示「嘿，別亂講」，或「嘿，別開我玩笑」。

說得漂亮--實況會話

●問路的時候，記得這樣說。

W　Excuse me. Which way to the rest room?

M　Third door on your left.

> W 請問，洗手間往哪裡走？
> M 你的左邊第三個門。

●不小心踩到對方的腳，對方叫了起來，你可以這樣說。

W　Ouch!

M　*Excuse me.* I didn't see you there.

W 唉呀！

M 對不起，我沒看到你在那裡。

●說「借過」的英語很容易。

W Excuse me. I'd like to get through here.

M Oh, sorry about that.

W 對不起，請讓路，我想過去。
M 噢，對不起。

●聽不懂時，這樣說最簡單。

W What time is it?

M *Excuse me?*

W I asked you what time it is.

W 幾點了？
M 你説什麼？
W 我問你，現在幾點。

●打擾別人時，這樣的口氣很客氣。

W John, sorry to bother you, but I need help with my research paper.

Jill referred me to you.

M No bother.
I've finished my work for the day, and I was just relaxing anyway.

Ⓦ 約翰，很抱歉打擾你，但是，我的研究報告需要
有人幫忙。
吉爾介紹我來找你。

Ⓜ 沒問題。
我今天的工作已經做完了，我只是在休息而已。

Tip !---英語小知識

Sorry to bother you, but...

通常我們若是有事情想請對方幫忙，在提出要求前先說
聲「不好意思，要打擾你」，對方總是比較不好意思拒
絕，英語的說法就是 Sorry to bother you, but...，在
but這個字的後面，把你要對方幫忙的事情說出來。

快熟句型---記住真好用

- Excuse me, where can I find indoor plants?
請問，我到哪裡可以找到室內植物？

- Excuse me, how do I get to the train station?
請問，到火車站怎麼走？

- Excuse me, but are you Miss Lin?
請問，你是林小姐嗎？

- Excuse me, I didn't see you there.
對不起，我沒看到你在那裡。

- Excuse me, did I spell your name wrong?

  對不起，我是否把你的名字拼錯了？

- Excuse me, guys, I'll be right back.

  對不起，各位，我馬上回來。

- Sorry to bother you, but could you tell me where the fitting rooms are?

  對不起，打擾了，但是，你可否告訴我，試衣間在哪裡？

超實用單字---1秒就記住

way [we]	（名）方向
rest room	（公共場所的）廁所；洗手間
left [lɛft]	（名）左邊
bother [ˈbaðɚ]	（動）打擾；困擾
research [ˈrisɝtʃ ; rɪˈsɝtʃ]	（名）研究
refer [rɪˈfɝ]	（動）叫～求助於～
finish [ˈfɪnɪʃ]	（動）完成
relaxing [rɪˈlæksɪŋ]	（形）放輕鬆
indoor [ˈɪnˌdor]	（形）室內的
plant [plænt]	（名）植物
spell [spɛl]	（動）拼字
wrong [rɔŋ]	（形）錯誤的

6. I beg your pardon.
請原諒。

Oops, I beg your pardon.

文法句型解說

I beg your pardon.

注意：pardon 這個字的用法，在很多方面跟 excuse 的用法很像，例如：當你做了什麼事，你覺得這件事有點不禮貌，或不小心犯了什麼錯，真正要向對方道歉時，可以說Excuse me. 來向對方表示歉意，也可以說 I beg your pardon. 來表示道歉。

例如：當你不小心撞到別人，或是不小心踩到別人的腳，你要跟對方說對不起，你可以說 I beg your pardon. 這是較正式且很有禮貌的說法，一般你也可以說，Excuse me. 或是 I'm sorry.

I beg your pardon?

在說明 Excuse me. 的用法時，我們說過，如果對方說的話你沒有聽清楚，你想要對方再說一遍時，你可以說，Excuse me?，同樣地，你也可以說 I beg your pardon? 或是把「I」省略掉，只說 Beg your pardon? 這種說法是較正式且很有禮貌的說法。

I beg your pardon?

我們在前一單元說過，當對方說了一句話，或說了一件事情，而你覺得對方的說法不禮貌，或是你覺得對方說的話，你不同意，你覺得對方在亂講時，你都可以說句「Excuse me?」表示「嘿，你不要開玩笑」，或「嘿，你不要亂講」。實際上，在這種情形下，你除了說 Excuse me? 之外，也可以說 I beg your pardon?
有時，對方說的話是在開你玩笑，而你也知道對方是在開你玩笑，你還是得抗議一聲，表示「嘿，別亂講」，或「嘿，別開我玩笑」，這種情形你也是要說 Excuse me? 或「I beg your pardon?」

說得漂亮--實況會話

●聽不懂時，也可以這樣說。

[W] I think the phone is not working.

[M] *I beg your pardon?*

[W] The telephone, I think it's not working.

[W] 電話好像不通。
[M] 你說什麼？

W 電話，我想電話是壞了。

●不小心撞到別人或弄倒別人的東西時，可以這樣說。

M Oops, I beg your pardon.

W No harm done.

M 糟了，對不起。
W 沒關係，沒弄壞什麼東西。

●不確定對方說什麼，可以這樣說。

W I'm going to quit my job.

M *I beg your pardon*, are you serious?

W 我想要辭職。
M 你說什麼，你不是說真的吧？

快熟句型---記住真好用

- I beg your pardon, I thought you were someone else.
  對不起，我認錯人了。

- I beg your pardon, I never said that at all.
  別亂講話，我從來沒那麼說。

超實用單字---1秒就記住

pardon [ˈpɑrdn̩]　　　　　(名)原諒　(動)原諒

beg [bɛg]	（動）請求
harm [hɑrm]	（名）傷害
quit [kwɪt]	（動）辭職；終止
job [dʒɑb]	（名）工作；職位；職務
serious [ˈsɪrɪəs]	（形）認真的；嚴肅的

Run that by me again.

文法句型解說

Run that by me again.

前面的單元裡，我們說過，若是有人跟你說話，你沒聽清楚，你要對方再說一遍，比較正式的說法是 I beg your pardon? 或 Beg your pardon?，而比較輕鬆的說法，則可以說 Run that by me again.

I didn't catch that.

當你沒聽清楚對方說的話時，你也可以跟對方說 I didn't catch that. 或是 I didn't get it.

Could you please repeat that?

這句話是請對方重說一遍，較正式、客氣的說法。

Would you say that again more slowly, please?

當對方說英語時，通常都是因為他說得太快，所以你沒聽清楚，如果你只是請他再重說一次，他還是說得那麼快，你仍然可能會聽不懂，你最好請他重說一遍，並要他說慢一點，那你就得記住這句話：Would you say that again more slowly, please?

What did you say?

你沒聽清楚對方說的話，你要問他「你說什麼啊？」英語就是 What did you say?；由於他說的話已經說過了，所以你這句話其實是問「你剛剛說什麼啊？」因此助動詞要用過去式助動詞「did」。

Come again?

你沒聽清楚對方說的話，你要請他重說一次，你可以跟他說「Come again」，是很乾淨俐落地說「再說一遍」的意思。

What?

你沒聽清楚對方說的話，最簡單的說法就是問對方「What?」對方就知道你沒聽清楚。

●當你聽不清楚別人說的話時，你可以這麼說，請對方再說一次。

W Do you have an English today?

M *Run that by me again.*

　　W 你今天有英文課嗎？
　　M 再說一遍。

●不知道別人在說什麼時的說法。

W Can you turn the TV down?

M What? What did you say?

　　W 你可以把電視的音量關小嗎？
　　M 什麼？ 你說什麼？

快熟句型---記住真好用

- Would you mind repeating what you just said?

  你介意把你剛剛說的再說一遍嗎？

- Could you please repeat what you just said?

  請你把你剛剛說的，再說一遍。

- Would you say that again more slowly, please?

  請你再說一遍，請說慢一點。

- Could you explain it again, a little slower please?

  請你再解釋一遍,請說慢一點。

- I beg your pardon?

  我沒聽清楚,請再說一遍。

- Beg your pardon?

  請再說一遍。

- What did you say?

  你剛剛說什麼?

- I didn't catch that.

  我沒聽清楚。

- Run that by me again.

  再說一遍。

- What?

  你說什麼?

超實用單字---1秒就記住

run [rʌn]	（動）（話語等）表達
catch [kætʃ]	（動）跟上並理解
repeat [rɪˈpit]	（動）重複
slowly [ˈsloli]	（副）慢慢地

mind [maɪnd]	（動）介意
explain [ɪk'splen]	（動）解釋
slower ['sloɚ]	（形）慢一點（slow的比較級）

8. I'm a very light sleeper.
我睡覺很容易醒。

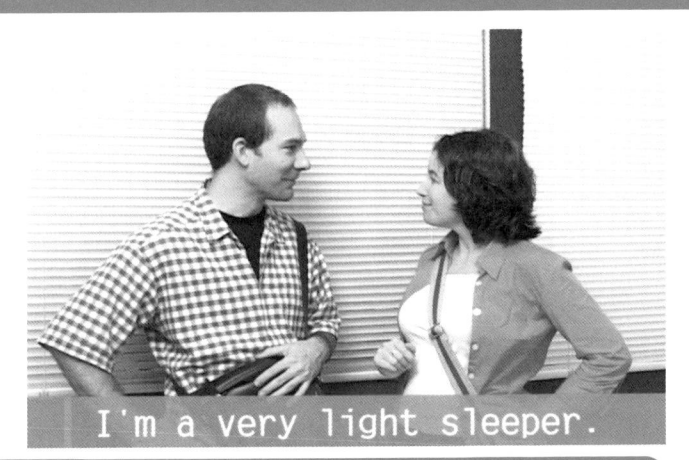

I'm a very light sleeper.

文法句型解說

a light sleeper

light 的意思是「輕輕的」，所以如果有一個人在睡覺時，總是睡得很輕，也就是睡不沈，聽到一點點小的聲音就會醒來，那麼我們就說這個人是 a light sleeper。

a heavy sleeper

heavy 的意思是「很重的」，如果有一個人是 a heavy sleeper，就是說這個人一旦睡著了，就會睡得很沈，再大的聲音也吵不醒他。

a sound sleeper

a sound sleeper 跟 a heavy sleeper不太一樣，sound 的意思是「很好的」，所以如果有一個人是 a sound sleeper，那就是說他總是能夠睡得很熟、睡得很好，不會一整夜翻來覆去、睡不安穩。

sleepyhead

當你看到一個人一副很愛睡的樣子時，你就可以叫他 sleepyhead，尤其是在早上，你要叫醒某人時，就可以說，Wake up, sleepyhead. 該起床了，貪睡鬼。

sleep over

在別人家過夜的英語就是「sleep over at ＋ 某人家」。

說得漂亮--實況會話

●很容易醒，可以這樣表達。

[W] Well, tomorrow is the big picnic.

[M] Oh, boy. I can hardly wait.

[W] The bus leaves early — at seven sharp.

[M] I'll have to get up by six.

[W] I'll ring your bell.

[M] No, don't do that.
 I don't want to awaken the others.

[W] I'll just toss a stone into your window.

[M] That will wake me up.

I'm a very light sleeper.

W 明天就是野餐的大日子。
M 噢,我實在等不及。

W 校車很早就要出發,是七點整。
M 我六點以前一定得起床。

W 我來按你家的門鈴。
M 不,不要按門鈴。
　　我不想吵醒其他人。

W 我會從窗口丟一個石頭到你的房間裡。
M 那就可以把我叫醒。
　　我很容易醒的。

Tip !---英語小知識

at seven sharp

當你跟別人約時間,你要強調是幾點整準時,不要超過時間,英語就是用 sharp 這個字,放在幾點的後面,例如:你要跟對方說約定的時間是「七點整」,英語就是「seven o'clock sharp」,你也可以把 o'clock 省略,只要說「seven sharp」就可以了。

● 到別人家過夜,這麼說最道地。

M Mom, can I sleep over at John's house?
W No, you can't sleep over.

M 媽,我可以到約翰家過夜嗎?
W 不行,你不可以去過夜。

- I'm a very light sleeper.
  我很容易醒的。

- I'm a sound sleeper.
  我睡覺都睡得很好。

- Come on sleepyhead, wake up.
  起床了，貪睡鬼。

- If you don't want to drive, you're welcome to sleep over.
  如果你今晚不想開車，可以在我家過夜。

超實用單字---1秒就記住

picnic [ˈpɪknɪk]	（名）野餐
hardly [ˈhɑrdlɪ]	（副）幾乎不
early [ˈɝlɪ]	（副）早
sharp [ʃɑrp]	（副）正（指時刻）
ring [rɪŋ]	（動）按門鈴
awaken [əˈwekən]	（動）吵醒
toss [tɔs]	（動）投；擲
sound [saʊnd]	（副）很好地
drive [draɪv]	（動）開車

9. I can sleep in this morning.
今早我可以睡晚一點。

Oh no! I overslept.

文法句型解說

sleep in

如果你平常都是每天早上六點起床，到了星期天，你就睡晚一點，睡到九點，那你就是在星期天 sleep in，換句話說，sleep in 的意思就是，睡得比平常起床的時間晚一點起來。注意： sleep in 不是「睡得太晚」的意思，而是因為放假或是不用上班，你想要睡得晚一點。

oversleep, overslept

你如果睡過頭了，也就是說你六點就應該起床，但是因為鬧鐘沒響，或是其他別的原因而睡得太晚，英語的說法不是 sleep late，而是 oversleep。當你告訴別人，你起得太晚的時候，由於「你起得太晚」這件事已經是過

去的事情了，所以通常說這句話的時候，都是用過去式動詞 overslept，整句話的說法就是 I overslept.

sleep like a log

在上一單元我們說過，一個人如果可以睡得很沈、睡得很好，我們就說他是一個 sound sleeper 或 heavy sleeper，我們也可以形容得生動一些，可以說 sleep like a log。說英語好玩的地方，在於罵人不帶髒字，中國人說別人睡得很沈，是說「睡得跟豬一樣」，而英語用 log（木頭）來形容，字面上像是文雅不少，其實講的是睡得一動也不動，像個「死人」似的。

sleep through...

如果昨晚半夜裡雷雨交加，而你竟然一點都不知道，也就是說你睡得很熟，暴風雨的聲音並沒有把你吵醒，當大家在說昨晚的暴風雨真大，閃電很嚇人時，你就可以說：

I didn't hear the storm.
我並沒有聽到暴風雨的聲音。
I guess I slept through it.
我想我睡得太熟了，暴風雨並沒有把我吵醒。

sleep on...

如果大家有一件事情要你做決定，你沒辦法馬上做決定，要想一個晚上再看看，英語的說法就是：

I don't know.
我現在不能做決定。
Let me sleep on it.

我想一個晚上看看。

●可以好好地睡個大頭覺，是很幸福的。

[W] Hey, I heard your boss gave you the day off tomorrow.

[M] I know.
I am really looking forward to sleeping in.

[W] 嘿，我聽說你明天不用上班。
[M] 是的。
我真的希望明天能夠晚一點起床。

●睡過頭，麻煩就大了。

[W] Honey, don't you have to be at work in ten minutes?

[M] Oh no! I overslept.
My boss is going to be angry with me.

[W] Don't worry.
He knows you've had a very hectic week.

[W] 親愛的，你不是還有十分鐘就得上班了？
[M] 噢，糟了，我睡過頭了。
我老闆一定會很生氣。

W 別擔心。
他知道你這個星期很忙。

- Today is my day off.
  今天是我的休假日。

- I really want to sleep in this morning.
  我今天早上真的想晚一點起床。

- I slept in both Saturday and Sunday.
  我星期六和星期天都很晚起床。

- John likes to sleep in on Sundays.
  約翰星期天喜歡晚起。

- Nothing can wake him up.
  沒有什麼事情可以叫醒他。

- He usually sleeps like a log.
  他通常都睡得很熟。

- I overslept this morning.
  我今早太晚起床了。

- I didn't hear the storm.
  我並沒有聽到暴風雨的聲音。

- I guess I slept through it.

我想我睡得很熟，暴風雨並沒有把我吵醒。

超實用單字---1秒就記住

heard [hɝd]	（動）聽見（hear的過去式）
boss [bɔs]	（名）主管；老闆
really [ˈrilɪ]	（副）真的
overslept [ˈovɚˈslɛpt]	（動）睡過頭了（oversleep的過去式）
worry [ˈwɝɪ]	（動）憂慮；擔心
hectic [ˈhɛktɪk]	（形）繁忙的；忙亂的
slept [slɛpt]	（動）睡（sleep的過去式）
usually [ˈjuʒʊəlɪ]	（副）通常
storm [stɔrm]	（名）暴風雨
guess [gɛs]	（動）猜想

10. Did I awaken you?

我把你吵醒了嗎？

Oh, did I awaken you?

文法句型解說

Did I awaken you?

awaken 當動詞，是「叫醒某人」或是「吵醒某人」的意思，例如：你打電話給某人，當對方來聽電話時，你聽到他還沒睡醒的聲音，你猜他可能在睡覺，被你的電話聲吵醒，你就可以問他說 Did I awaken you?（我把你吵醒了嗎？）awaken 的過去式和過去分詞是 awakened。

wake 某人up

wake 當動詞時，通常與 up 連用，意思是「叫醒某人」，或是「吵醒某人」，例如：嬰孩在睡覺，你吩咐其他的人不要把他吵醒，英語的說法就是：

The baby is sleeping.
Don't wake him up.

awake

awake 當形容詞，是「醒著」的意思，例如：你躺在床上，你的朋友進來，問你是否醒著，英語的說法就是 Are you awake?，而你要跟他說「是的，我醒著」，英語的說法就是 Yes, I'm awake.

awake

awake 當動詞時，意思是「醒來」，它的過去式是 awoke，過去分詞是 awoken。
它是個不及物動詞，也就是說 awake 這個動詞後面不接受詞，說明的是某個人醒了，例如：
The baby awoke and began to cry.
嬰孩醒了，就開始哭。

說得漂亮--實況會話

●把別人吵醒了，可不太好。

W　Hey John, what are you doing?

M　I was sleeping.

W　Oh, did I awaken you?

M　Actually, you did.
　　What did you need?

W Nothing, really.

I just called to talk.

M Well then, if it's nothing important, call me later.

I'm going back to bed.

W 嘿，約翰，你在做什麼？
M 我剛剛在睡覺。

W 噢，我把你吵醒了嗎？
M 是的。
    你打電話來有什麼事？

W 也沒什麼事。
    我只是打電話來聊天。

M 那，如果沒什麼重要的事，以後再打給我。
    我要回去睡覺了。

●有些人不叫是不會起床的。

W Where is John?

M He's sleeping.

W Well, wake him up.

It's time to go.

M Okay, I'll go get him up.

W 約翰在哪裡？
M 他在睡覺。

W 那，把他叫醒。
該走了。

M 好，我去叫他起床。

●問別人是否醒著，就這麼問。

W John?

M What?

W Are you awake?

M I am now. What do you need?

W 約翰？

M 什麼事？

W 你醒著嗎？

M 我現在醒了。有什麼事？

快熟句型---記住真好用

- The noise outside awakened him.
  外面的吵聲把他吵醒了。

- Did I awaken you?
  我把你吵醒了嗎？

- Mary is sleeping. Don't wake her up.
  瑪麗在睡覺，不要把她吵醒。

- Are you awake?
  你醒著嗎？

- The baby awoke and began to cry.
  嬰孩醒了，就開始哭。

wake [wek]	（動）吵醒
actually [ˈæktʃʊəlɪ]	（副）實際上；事實上
really [ˈrilɪ]	（副）真的
important [ɪmˈpɔrtənt]	（形）重要的
later [ˈletɚ]	（副）稍後
awake [əˈwek]	（副）醒著的 （動）醒來
awoke [əˈwok]	（動）醒來（awake的過去式）
noise [nɔɪz]	（名）雜音；噪音
awaken [əˈwekən]	（動）叫醒
cry [kraɪ]	（動）哭

11. The traffic seems very light today.
今天的交通看起來不擁擠。

It is very light.

文法句型解說

light

light 這個字有很多意思，大家學過的是「天亮」的意思，例如：我們說「在夏天大約四點半，天就亮了。」英語的說法就是：

It gets light at about 4:30 in the summer.

又如：到了晚上八點多，我們要說「外面天還是亮的。」英語的說法就是 It is still light outside.

light

light 有另一個大家熟悉的意思，就是「輕的」，如果你

在搬東西，有人想要來幫忙，你要跟他說「你可以拿這個袋子，這個很輕。」英語的說法就是 You can carry this bag. It is very light.

light

上一單元我們學過一個睡覺睡不沈、一點點聲音就會醒的人，是一個 light sleeper。

light meal

light 也可以做「少量」的意思，所以如果你吃飯時，不想吃很多，你就可以說你只想要個 light meal 或 light lunch。

light 當「少量」的意思時，也可以用在說明交通流量，如果我們說：「今天的交通流量不大，不太擁擠。」英語的說法就是 The traffic seems very light today.

light smoker

若一個人抽煙但是抽得不多，我們就說他是一個 light smoker。同樣地，一個人吃飯都吃得很少量，英語就說他是個 light eater。

說得漂亮--實況會話

●塞不塞車、交通好不好，就是這麼說。

[W] How bad is the traffic today?

[M] It's not bad at all.

It seems very light.

W That's good.

I don't feel like fighting the traffic this morning.

M You shouldn't have any trouble at all.

W 今天的交通有多糟？

M 今天的交通一點都不糟。
車輛蠻少的。

W 那很好。
今早我可不想在亂糟糟的交通裡開車。

M 你應該不會有什麼問題。

Tip !---英語小知識

light

light 的相反詞是 heavy，所以，交通不擁擠的英語是 light，交通很擁擠的英語就是 heavy。

同樣地，一個人抽煙抽得不多，是一個 light smoker，一個抽煙抽得很多的人就是一個 heavy smoker，而一個人若是喝酒喝得很凶，那他就是一個 heavy drinker。

● 說天是亮的還是黑的，這樣說就對了。

W How dark is it outside?

M Actually, it's still light.

W That's great.

I need to shoot these pictures before it gets dark.

[M] Well, you still have an hour before the sun goes down.

[W] 外面天多黑？
[M] 事實上，天還很亮。

[W] 那很好。
我需要在天黑前，拍這些照片。
[M] 嗯，太陽下山前，你還有一個小時的時間。

●表達東西很輕，太簡單了。

[M] Mommy, I want to help carry the bags.
[W] You can carry this one.

It is very light.

[M] I can carry that one, too.
[W] That's okay, I've got it.

Just carry the light one and be careful not to drop it.

[M] 媽，我想幫你拿這些袋子。
[W] 你可以拿這一個。
這個很輕。

[M] 我也可以拿那一個。
[W] 沒關係，這個我拿就好。
你只要拿那個輕的，小心別掉了。

- The traffic seems very light today.
  今天的交通似乎不太擁擠。

- It gets light at about 4:30 in the summer.
  夏天，四點半天就亮了。

- It is still light outside.
  外面天還是亮的。

- The sun makes this room very light.
  太陽使得這個房間很亮。

- The room is light and airy.
  這個房間光線好又通風。

- A bag of feathers is very light.
  一袋的羽毛很輕。

- He has grown much weaker and is now capable of only light work.
  他變得更虛弱，現在只能做輕便的工作。

超實用單字---1秒就記住

traffic [ˈtræfɪk]		（名）交通
seem [sim]		（動）似乎
light [laɪt]		（形）輕的；亮的；少量的；易醒的

trouble [ˈtrʌbl̩]	（名）麻煩；困難
dark [dɑrk]	（形）天黑的
shoot [ʃut]	（名）拍照；拍攝
picture [ˈpɪktʃɚ]	（名）照片
carry [ˈkærɪ]	（動）攜帶
careful [ˈkɛrfəl]	（形）小心的；仔細的
drop [drɑp]	（動）掉下；丟下；拋下
room [rum]	（名）房間；空間
airy [ˈɛrɪ]	（形）通風的
feather [ˈfɛðɚ]	（名）羽毛
weaker [ˈwikɚ]	（形）越來越弱的（weak的比較級）
capable [ˈkepəbl̩]	（形）有能力的

12. I want a second helping.

我還要再來一份。

No, I would like a second helping.

文法句型解說

a second helping

吃飯時，你拿的一份菜，或是別人或服務生拿給你的一份菜，就叫做一個 helping。如果你的一份吃完了，要再拿第二份，那就是 a second helping，例如：去吃自助餐，當你吃完了第一份之後，你要再去拿第二份，英語的說法就是：

I'm going to get a second helping.
我要去拿第二份。

May I have seconds?

用餐時，如果你覺得很好吃，想要再來一份，英語可以說 a second helping，也可以說 seconds，所以想再來一份，你就可以問說 May I have seconds? 。如果你是主人，問吃飯的客人要不要再來一份，你就可以這樣問客人：

Does anyone want seconds?
有沒有人要再來一份？

說得漂亮--實況會話

●想要再來一份，可以這樣說。

[W] Are you finished, sir?

[M] No, I would like a second helping of the steak and potatoes.

[W] 先生，你吃完了嗎？
[M] 還沒，我還要再來一份牛排和馬鈴薯。

Tip !---英語小知識

Are you finished
問對方「該做的事情做完了嗎」，或是「飯吃完了嗎」，英語的說法是 Are you finished? 或 Are you done?

●請人再上一份，就這樣說。

[M] Excuse me.

Can you bring a second helping of the turkey, please?

[W] Right away, sir.

[M] 對不起。
　　請你再拿一份火雞肉來好嗎？
[W] 馬上來。

●問人家要不要再來一份，就是這樣問。

[W] Would you like a second helping or should I bring the check?

[M] Check, please.
I've had my fill for tonight.

[W] 你還要再來一份嗎，還是你要結帳了？
[M] 我要結帳了。
　　我已經吃飽了。

Tip !---英語小知識

have my fill

I have my fill. 的意思是「我已經吃了我能吃的量」，也就是「吃得很飽的意思」。如果你要說「我這一頓飯已經吃得夠多了」，也就是說「我已經吃得很飽了」，英語除了說 I'm full. 或 I'm stuffed. 以外，還可以說 I've had my fill.

●想再吃一份，這樣說就對了。

> **M** You know what, I think I'm going to get a second helping.

> **W** Would you get me one, too please?

> **M** 我想我還要再去拿一份。
> **W** 請你也幫我拿一份，好嗎？

**快熟句型---記住真好用**

- Can I have a second helping?
  我可以再吃一份嗎？

- I'm going to get a second helping.
  我要去拿第二份。

- I can never get my fill of shrimp. I love them.
  我喜歡蝦子，吃再多也不夠。

- I've had my fill for tonight.
  我今晚吃得很飽了。

- I'm full.
  我吃飽了。

- I'm stuffed.
  我吃得很飽。

- Thanks. You've been a big help.

謝謝你，你真的幫了很大的忙。

Tip !---英語小知識

a big help

a big help 這個慣用語的意思是「一個很有幫助的人」，或是「一個幫了很多忙的人」。在某一個人幫忙你很多之後，你要謝謝對方並説「你真的幫了我很多忙」，英語的説法是 Thanks. You've been a big help.

- Are you finished?

你做完了嗎？

- Are you finished with your project?

你的研究作業做完了嗎？

- We will fill up at the next little town.

到下一個城鎮，我們就要把油加滿。

Tip !---英語小知識

fill up

把車子的油加滿的英語是 fill up。例如：你們開車出外旅行，途中油箱快沒有油了，你説「我必須停下來把油加滿，因為油箱快沒油了」，英語的説法是 I've got to stop and fill up. I'm running low.

finished [ˈfɪnɪʃt]	（動）完成了（finish的過去分詞）
helping [ˈhɛlpɪŋ]	（名）（食物的）一份；一客
steak [stek]	（名）牛排
potato [pəˈteto]	（名）馬鈴薯
second [ˈsɛkənd]	（形）第二的
turkey [ˈtɝkɪ]	（名）火雞
check [tʃɛk]	（動）帳單
fill [fɪl]	（動）充分；足夠
shrimp [ʃrɪmp]	（動）蝦
stuffed [stʌft]	（形）塞飽肚皮；使吃得很飽
project [ˈprɑdʒɛkt]	（名）專案；企畫
town [taʊn]	（名）城市；城鎮

13. I'm full.
我飽了。

No, thank you. I'm full.

文法句型解說

I'm full.

當你吃完飯，你說「我吃飽了」，英語的說法就是 I'm full.

I'm stuffed.

stuff 這個字當動詞，就是「裝填東西」的意思，stuffed 是個形容詞，指「吃得很飽的」意思。如果你已經吃得很飽，再也吃不下任何東西了，就可以說 I'm stuffed.

I'm starving.

starving 當形容詞，意思是「快餓死了」。所以當你肚子很餓的時候，英語的說法就是，I'm starving.

● 吃飽了，就這麼說。

[W] John, would you like some more soup?
We have plenty.

[M] No, thank you. I'm full.
It's been a wonderful dinner.

[W] 約翰，你還要再來一些湯嗎？
我們還有很多。
[M] 不用，謝謝你，我已經飽了。
這頓晚餐真好吃。

● 吃飽了，還可以這樣說。

[W] John, we've got dessert next if you can
stay awhile.

[M] Thanks, but no.
I'm stuffed and I need to be heading
home.

[W] 約翰，你如果能多留一會兒，接下去要吃甜點。
[M] 謝謝你，但是不用了。
我已經吃飽了，而且我也該回家了。

Tip !---英語小知識

head home

head 做動詞，可以做「朝某個方向去」的意思，所
以當你說要回家時，就可以說是 head home，例如：

「我該回家了」，整句英語的說法是 I need to be heading home.

●要留肚子吃其他東西，該怎麼說？

M　Mary, your roast beef is marvelous.

W　I've got more if you'd like.

M　I've had plenty, thanks.
Besides, I have to leave some room for your apple pie.

M 瑪麗，你的烤牛肉真好吃。

W 如果你還要吃，我還有。

M 謝謝你，我已經吃了很多。
而且，我還要留一些肚子吃你的蘋果派。

Tip !---英語小知識

room

room 最常見的意思是「房間」，這個字也可以當「抽象的空間」的意思，例如：你到朋友家吃飯，他問你要不要再來一碗，你說你想留一點肚子吃甜點，也就是說你想要你的肚子留下點「空間」來吃甜點，這裡的空間，英語就是用 room 這個字，整句英語的說法是 I have to leave some room for dessert.

- No, no dessert, I'm stuffed.
  不用，不用甜點，我已經飽了。

- I'm starving.
  我餓壞了。

- I need to be heading home.
  我必須要回家了。

- Where are you guys headed?
  你們要去哪裡？

be headed

在英語會話中，head 當動詞，表示「朝某個方向去」的意思時，也常用 be headed 的說法，例如：你看到你的朋友們要出去，你想知道他們要去什麼地方，你就可以問他們Where are you guys headed?（你們要去哪裡？）

- There is apple pie for dessert.
  有蘋果派當甜點。

- I have to leave some room for dessert.
  我需要留點肚子吃甜點。

full [fʊl]	（形）吃飽；滿的
stuffed [stʌft]	（形）填滿的
starving [ˈstɑrvɪŋ]	（形）很餓
soup [sup]	（名）湯
wonderful [ˈwʌndɚfəl]	（形）好棒的；絕妙的；好極了
dessert [dɪˈzɝt]	（名）（飯後）甜點
head [hɛd]	（動）往某個方向前進
roast [rost]	（形）烤好的
marvelous [ˈmɑrvl̩əs]	（形）很棒的
plenty [ˈplɛntɪ]	（名）很多
besides [bɪˈsaɪdz]	（副）除此之外

14. I get it.
我聽懂了。

I get it!

文法句型解說

I get it.

get 這個字可以當「瞭解」的意思。當大家在聊天，你對某人所說的話一時會意不過來，思索了一會兒，你知道他說什麼了，這時候你就可以說，I get it.

或是有人說了一個笑話，你剛開始聽不懂，有人解釋給你聽，或是你自己思考了一下之後聽懂了，你同樣可以說 I get it.

I don't get it.

get 當「瞭解」的意思時，它的否定片語 not get it 的意思就是「不瞭解」。當你對某種情形有疑問、有不瞭解的地方，好像大家這麼做或是這麼說並不太合情理

時，你就可以說 I don't get it.。或是某個人說了一個笑話，你聽不懂時，就可以說 I don't get it.。

又例如：某人說了一個笑話，大夥兒笑彎了腰，唯獨約翰一個人，一副茫茫然的樣子，有人解釋給他聽，他還是聽不懂，這個人只好搖搖頭說：

He just didn't get it.

他就是聽不懂。

說得漂亮--實況會話

●當你終於知道了問題的答案或了解某件事時，這麼說最口語。

W I get it! The answer is "Egypt"

M Yeah, you get it. Nice job!

W 我知道了！答案是「埃及」。
M 沒錯，你答對了。真不賴！

●聽不懂或看不懂時，可以這麼說。

M It's a joke? I dont't get it.

W I know. You just didnt't get it.

M 這是個笑話嗎？我不懂。
W 我知道。你就是不懂。

快熟句型---記住真好用

● He just didn't get it.
他就是聽不懂。

- She still doesn't get what the movie's about.

  她還是不知道這部電影在演什麼。

15. Do you follow?
你聽得懂嗎？

Do you follow?

文法句型解說

Do you follow?

follow 這個字當「動詞」，可以當「瞭解別人說的話」，或是「瞭解別人的說明」，或是「瞭解小說或故事的情結」的意思，所以當你在說明一件事情，或是交代工作，或是指路，有時你會停下來問一下對方，是否聽懂你所說的，英語的問法就是 Do you follow?

Do you know what I'm saying?

在你說話的當中，若你想問對方是否聽懂你說的話，除了用 Do you follow? 之外，你也可以用 Do you know what I'm saying? 或 Do you know what I mean?

注意：說英語時，用疑問句問對方時，正式的問法是「Do you + 你要問的？」，但在口語中的說法則常常會把 Do 省略掉，就問 You know what I'm saying? 或 You know what I mean? 就好了。

I couldn't follow you.

Do you follow? 是用來問對方有沒有聽懂你說的話，如果對方說的話你沒完全聽懂，你就可以跟他說 I couldn't follow you. 或是 I couldn't quite follow you.

說得漂亮--實況會話

●問人家聽懂了沒，可以這樣問。

[W] Take a left at the light on Main street, go about half a mile, and then turn right.

Do you follow?

[M] No. Run it by me again.

> [W] 在緬因街的紅綠燈處向左轉，走大約半哩路，右轉。
>
> 聽得懂嗎？
>
> [M] 沒聽懂，再說一次。

●問人家聽懂了沒，這樣問更簡潔。

[W] Please make a copy of this letter.

Put the letter in the file and send the

copy to Mr. Smith.

Got that?

Ⓜ I've got it.

    Ⓦ 請你把這封信複印一份。

       這封信歸檔，把影印本寄給史密斯先生。

       聽懂了嗎？

    Ⓜ 聽懂了。

快熟句型---記住真好用

- Do you know what I'm saying?
  你知道我在說什麼嗎？

- Do you follow?
  你有沒有聽懂？

- I couldn't follow you.
  我沒聽懂你說什麼。

- I couldn't quite follow you.
  我聽不太懂你說什麼。

- I didn't quite follow what he was saying.
  他說什麼，我聽不太懂。

- I must admit I found the plot a bit hard to follow.
  我必須承認，我發現這個情節有點難瞭解。

- I've got it.

 我懂了。

超實用單字---1秒就記住

light [laɪt]	（名）交通燈；紅綠燈
mile [maɪl]	（名）哩
left [lɛft]	（名）左邊
right [raɪt]	（名）右邊
follow [ˈfɑlo]	（動）理解
copy [ˈkɑpɪ]	（名）副本
file [faɪl]	（名）檔案
send [sɛnd]	（動）寄；送
admit [ədˈmɪt]	（動）承認
hard [hɑrd]	（形）困難的

16. Do you get the message?

你知道人家在暗示什麼嗎？

Get the message?

文法句型解說

get the message

get 這個動詞有很多意思，在英語會話中也可以當「瞭解」的意思。get the message 這個片語的意思就是「聽得懂對方暗示性的話」，例如：你想跟對方一起去逛街，但是對方卻說「外面太冷了，你別去」，或是「我去一下就回來，你不用去」等等一些你認為無關緊要的理由，講了半天，你總算瞭解他說來說去，最主要的原因就是不要你跟著去，這時你就可以回答他說：I get the message --- you just don't want me to come with you. （我知道你的意思，你就是不要我跟你去。）

Do you get the message?

當你不跟對方直接明說,而是用暗示的,然後你想知道對方是否聽得懂你暗示的話,或是你聽到瑪麗在跟約翰暗示一些話,你看約翰好像沒有聽出來瑪麗暗示的話,你就可以問他說,「你有沒有聽出來,別人在暗示你的話」,英語的說法就是 Do you get the message?

You get the message?

在講英語時,用疑問句問時不一定要把do說出來,所以 Do you get the message? 這句話可以只說 You get the message?

Do you get the picture?

picture 在這裡的意思是「事態;情況;局面」的意思。Do you get the picture? 這句話跟 Do you get the message? 這句話有點類似,只是 Do you get the message? 是用在問對方有沒有聽懂別人在暗示的話,而 Do you get the picture? 是用在問對方有沒有弄清楚目前的情況。

說得漂亮--實況會話

●暗示別人是否聽懂你給的訊息,記得這樣說。

W Stop following me around.

Get the message?

M I guess so.

W 不要到處跟著我。
你知道我的意思吧？

M 大概知道吧。

Tip !---英語小知識

I guess so.

當你要回答「是」，但又不想用很肯定的話回答，而是
要用有點不太在意，不是百分之百肯定的話回答時，英
語的說法是 I guess so.

●聽見沒有？在罵人或訓示人時，這句話可是常用到。

M I want you to study harder.
Do you hear?

W Sure, dad. Whatever you say.

M 我要你用功一點。
聽見沒有？

W 聽到了，爸，你怎麼說我就怎麼做。

Tip !---英語小知識

Do you hear?

當你要對方做某件事情，而且是要求對方一定要去做
時，通常會加問一句 Do you hear?。這句話很容易
懂，照字面的意思就是「你有沒有聽到？」，其實是在
強調你要對方一定要照你的話去做。

W I want you to clean up your room now.

  Do you hear?

M Okay. I'll get right on it.

  W 我要你現在就把你的房間整理乾淨。
   你聽到了嗎？

  M 好的，我馬上去做。

Tip !---英語小知識

I'll get right on it.
當你答應對方，你馬上會去做某件事情時，英語的說法
是 I'll get right on it.

快熟句型---記住真好用

- Do you get the message?
  你知道人家在暗示你什麼嗎？

- Do you get the picture?
  你搞清楚目前的情況沒有？

- I don't get it.
  我不明白。

I don't get it.

get 當「瞭解」的意思時，它的否定片語 not get it 的意思就是「不瞭解」，當你對某種情形有很多不瞭解的地方，你就可以說 I don't get it.，表示你對整個情況有疑問，有不瞭解的地方。或是某個人說了一個笑話，你聽不懂時，你就可以說 I don't get it.，表示你聽不懂。若是有人對你說明那句笑話的意思，你總算聽懂了，那你就可以回答他 I get it.，表示「我懂了」。

● **Do you hear?**
聽見沒有？

message [ˈmɛsɪdʒ]	（名）訊息	
follow [ˈfɑlo]	（動）跟隨	
around [əˈraʊnd]	（副）在旁邊	
picture [ˈpɪktʃɚ]	（名）事態；情況；局面	

17. You know what?
你知道嗎？／你知道嗎！

You know what?

文法句型解說

You know what?

You know what? 按照字面的意思就是「你知道什麼事嗎？」其實這句話是用在你要告訴對方一件事情或一個消息時，想要引起對方的興趣和注意而已，並不是真的要問對方知不知道什麼事情。You know what? 的用法和下一句Guess what! 的用法一樣。

Guess what!

Guess 這個字的意思是「猜猜看」，Guess what! 按照字面的意思就是「你猜猜看！」它的用法和You know what? 一樣，都是用來引起聽話者的興趣和注意而已。通常，對方在說了 Guess what! 之後，不等你回答就會

繼續把他要告訴你的消息迫不及待地說出來。

如果對方說了 Guess what! 之後，沒有繼續說下去，你只要順口回他「What?」就對了，問他「你有什麼消息要說呢？」

說得漂亮--實況會話

●「你知道嗎？」你是不是也常說這句口頭禪？

W You know what?

Mary and Jenny are back in town for the weekend.

M That's great.

I haven't seen them since graduation.

W Why don't we all get together and go to the movies or something?

M Sounds great.

Just give me a call.

W 你知道嗎？

瑪麗和珍妮回來度週末。

M 那好棒。

畢業後，我就沒看到她們了。

W 我們何不大家見個面，一起去看電影或是做什麼的？

M 好啊。

約好了，打個電話給我。

Sounds great.

當有人做了一個提議，而你同意時，你可以説 Sounds great. 來表示你同意對方的提議。

● 有好消息時，這樣說很能表達你的心情。

W　Guess what!

M　What?

W　I'm going to the United States this summer.

M　That's great.

W 你猜猜看！
M 什麼事？

W 我暑假要到美國去。
M 那很棒啊！

● 要引起人家注意時，這樣說很有效。

W　There you are, John.

I've been looking all over for you.

M　Well, you found me.
What's up?

W　Guess what!

I've a couple of tickets to the upcoming Madonna concert.

Want to come?

M **You know** I'd love to.

W 約翰，你在這裡。
   我到處在找你。

M 那，你找到了。
   有什麼事？

W 你猜猜我有什麼！
   我有兩張瑪丹娜將要開的演唱會的票。
   你要不要去？

M 你知道我會去的。

Tip !---英語小知識

What's up?

What's up? 這句話按照字面的意思是「有什麼事？」，在這個單元裡，這句話是問「有什麼事」的意思。

這句話也常用在兩個很熟的朋友見面時，打招呼的話。其實兩個朋友見了面，說這句話的本意是在問對方「近來有什麼事？」，所以熟朋友間不想文謅謅地問 How are you?，就可以說 What's up?

Want to come?

當你邀約對方一起去時，英語最簡單的說法就是 Want to come?。除了這個說法以外，也可以說 Do you want to come? 或 Would you like to come?

I'd love to.

當有人對你提出邀約時，如果你答應去，回答的説法是 I'd love to.

- We are going to the movies tonight.
  我們今晚要去看電影。

- Want to come?
  你要不要一起去？

- We'll have to get together sometime.
  我們偶爾應該聚一聚。

- When can we get together?
  我們什麼時候可以聚一聚？

超實用單字---1秒就記住

back [bæk]	（副）回來
town [taʊn]	（名）城市；城鎮
since [sɪns]	（連）自從
graduation [ˌgrædʒʊˈeʃən]	（名）畢業
summer [ˈsʌmɚ]	（名）夏天

found [faʊnd]	（動）找到（find的過去式）
guess [gɛs]	（動）猜想
concert [ˈkɑnsɚt]	（名）演奏會；音樂會
ticket [ˈtɪkɪt]	（名）票
couple [ˈkʌpl̩]	（名）一對；一雙
a couple of	兩張～

May I be excused?

文法句型解說

Could you excuse us, please?

當我們想請對方做某件事情時，你可以直截了當跟對方說「就這麼做」，但是美國人講話通常都是客客氣氣的，他們通常都會說：「請你做這件事，好嗎？」

前面的單元曾提到當一夥人在一起，而你要先告退或是要先離開一下時，就要跟大家說 Excuse me.。如果你們是幾個人要先行離開，當然要把 me 改成 us，要說 Excuse us.

除了可以直截了當的說 Excuse us. 之外，也可以用更客氣一點的說法：Could you excuse us, please?

Could I be excused?

當你要請求對方同意時，該使用的英語句型是：「May I + 你要對方同意的事？」，「Can I + 你要對方同意的事？」，和「Could I + 你要對方同意的事？」這三個句型。

當你要先告退或是要先離開一下時，除了可以說 Excuse me. 之外，還可以用更客氣的方式問「我要先離開，好嗎？」這句話裡含有「請求對方同意」的意思，所以你可以這樣說：Could I be excused? 或 May I be excused? 或 Can I be excused?

說得漂亮--實況會話

●要先離席時，記得這樣說，會顯得你很有禮貌。

[M] Mom, I'm full and I've got some stuff to do.

May I be excused?

[W] Finish your green beans and you may.

[M] 媽，我吃飽了，而且我還有事情要做。

我可以先離開嗎？

[W] 把綠豆吃完，你就可以先離開。

●有事要離開一下，就這麼說。

[W] I'm very sorry, but I've just received an urgent page on my beeper.

Excuse me for a moment.

M No problem.

W 很抱歉，我的傳呼機有人緊急在呼叫。
我先離開一下。

M 沒問題。

●要先行離開回家，你可以這樣說。

W Have you had fun tonight?

M It was a splendid party.
My wife is tired though, so we must be
getting home.

W 你今晚玩得愉快嗎？
M 真是很棒的宴會。
但是我太太累了，我們必須回家。
先告辭了。

快熟句型---記住真好用

● Could you excuse us, please?
對不起，我們先告退。

● Could I be excused?
我可以先告退嗎？

● May I be excused?
我可以先告退嗎？

full [fʊl]	（形）吃飽的
stuff [stʌf]	（名）事情
finish [ˈfɪnɪʃ]	（動）完成
green [grin]	（形）綠色的
bean [bin]	（名）豆；蠶豆
receive [rɪˈsiv]	（動）收到
urgent [ˈɝdʒənt]	（形）緊急的
page [pedʒ]	（名）呼叫
beeper [ˈbipɚ]	（名）呼叫器
moment [ˈmomənt]	（名）一瞬間；片刻
fun [fʌn]	（名）好玩；樂趣
splendid [ˈsplɛndɪd]	（形）極好的；極令人滿意的
tired [taɪrd]	（形）疲倦的
though [ðo]	（副）（口語）不過（放在句尾）

19. Could I get you something to drink?

你要喝什麼飲料嗎？

Just give me a cup of water.

文法句型解說

Could I...?

「Could I...?」這個句型通常是用在「請求對方的許可」時。當有客人到你家，你要問客人想喝什麼飲料時，中文的說法是「What do you want to drink? （你想喝什麼嗎？）」但是美國人通常不這麼說，他們都會很客氣的、帶點請求同意的口氣問說「Could I get you something to drink? （我可以拿什麼飲料給你喝嗎？）」 好像沒有得到你的同意，就拿飲料給你喝，是很不禮貌的事情似的，其實不是，這只是他們說話的方式而已，這句話真正的意思，還是在問客人想喝什麼飲料。

問客人想喝什麼飲料，也可以說 Would you care for a drink? 或簡單地說 Care for a drink?

Would you care for a drink?

當你對客人說 Would you care for a drink?，表示你有幾種飲料可以提供給你的客人喝，如果你想問他要不要喝可樂，你可以這樣說：Would you care for a coke? 同樣的句型也可以用來問「你要不要再來一杯？」英語的說法就是 Would you care for another one?

Would you prefer tea or coffee?

當你有兩種飲料可供對方選擇時，你就可以問他：「Would you prefer這種飲料or另一種飲料？」例如：你要問對方要喝茶還是咖啡時，英語的說法就是 Would you prefer tea or coffee? 或者你也可以說：Would you like tea or coffee?

如果你是在餐廳吃飯，點菜時，服務生在你點完菜之後，可能會問你要喝什麼飲料，這時他通常會說：Would you like a drink to go with that?，意思是說你吃飯時，要喝什麼飲料嗎？

說得漂亮--實況會話

●問人家要不要喝東西時，可以這樣問。

[W] It's very hot out here.

Would you care for a coke?

Ⓜ Yes, thank you.

Ⓦ 這裡真熱。
你要喝可樂嗎？
Ⓜ 好的，謝謝你。

●要提供服務時，就這麼問。

Ⓦ What can I get for you?

Ⓜ A cold lemonade sounds great right about now.

Ⓦ 你要我拿什麼給你嗎？
Ⓜ 現在來一杯冰檸檬汁應該很好。

●問人家是否要搭配飲料，就這麼說。

Ⓦ Would you like a drink to go with that?

Ⓜ No thanks. Just give me a cup of water.

Ⓦ 你要喝點什麼配這個嗎？
Ⓜ 不用。給我一杯水就可以了。

●坐飛機時，一定會聽到的一句話。

Ⓦ Would you like tea or coffee?

Ⓜ I think I'll have some coffee, please.

Ⓦ 你要茶還是咖啡？
Ⓜ 請給我咖啡。

I'll have...

當對方要拿飲料給你喝，問你「要喝這種飲料，還是另外一種飲料」 時，你可以用這個句型： 「I'll have + 你想要喝的飲料」，例如：對方問你 Would you prefer tea or coffee?，而你想喝咖啡，你就可以回答 I think I'll have coffee.

- Could I get you something to drink?
  你要我拿什麼飲料給你喝嗎？

What do you have?

如果對方要拿飲料給你喝，對你說 Could I get you something to drink? 時，你可以問他 What do you have?，因為在這種情形下，你可能不太清楚他有什麼飲料可以給你喝，所以你就問他「你有什麼飲料？」，等他告訴你他有什麼飲料時，你再從中挑選一樣。

當然，當他問你 Could I get you something to drink? 時，你也可以跟他說「我要可樂（I think I'll have coke.）」，如果他正好沒有可樂時，他會跟你說他有什麼，那你再決定也可以。

- Would you care for a coke?
  你要喝可樂嗎？

- Would you prefer tea or coffee?
  你要茶還是咖啡？

- Would you like tea or coffee?
  你要茶還是咖啡？

hot [hɑt]	（形）熱的
coke [kok]	（名）可樂
lemonade [ˌlɛmən'ed]	（名）檸檬汁
drink [drɪŋk]	（動）喝（飲料）（名）飲料；酒
tea [ti]	（名）茶

20. Could I have the check?

買單。

Could I have the check?

文法句型解說

Could I have the check?

前面提過「Could I...?」這個句型是用在「請求對方同意」時，不過有時美國人在提出要求時，也會用這個句型，表面上還是在請求對方的同意，但只是一種客氣的說法，實際上他是在提出要求，例如：在餐廳用完餐後，你要服務生把帳單給你，你可以說 Could I have the check?，表面上你是問服務生「我可以拿帳單嗎？」，實際上你是在跟服務生說「我要帳單，請把帳單拿給我。」

Check, please.

check 有兩種意思：支票；帳單。所以當你在餐廳裡聽見

Check, please. 時，可別誤以為顧客在向服務生要支票？
其實這句話的意思是要服務生把帳單給你。

要服務生把帳單給你，除了簡單地說 Check, please. 之
外，也可以更客氣地說 Could I have the check?

說得漂亮--實況會話

●聽懂服務生的這句話，吃飯就不成問題了。

[W] **Welcome to the Olive Garden.**

I can take your order now.

[M] **We'll start with the "Taste of Italy Special".**

Bring some peanuts, too.

[W] 歡迎到「橄欖園餐廳」。
你們可以點菜了。

[M] 先給我們「義大利特餐」。
順便拿炒花生來。

●要買單，可以說得很客氣。

[W] **Would you like some dessert tonight?**

[M] **I don't think so.**

Could I have the check?

[W] 你們今晚要吃甜點嗎？

[M] 不用。
請給我帳單。

- Could I have the check?
  請把帳單給我。

- Could I take your order now?
  你們要點菜了嗎？

order [ˈɔrdɚ]	（名）點菜（動）（動）點菜
start [stɑrt]	（動）開始
decide [dɪˈsaɪd]	（動）決定
dessert [dɪˈzɝt]	（名）（飯後）甜點
check [tʃɛk]	（名）帳單
figure [ˈfɪgjɚ]	（動）（口語）認為；想

Could I take a message?

文法句型解說

Can I speak to Mary?

英語中有三種句型用來提出要求，請求對方同意：「May I ＋ 你要對方同意的事？」，「Can I ＋ 你要對方同意的事？」，和「Could I ＋ 你要對方同意的事？」，所以打電話時，當接聽電話的人並不是你要找的人時，你要告訴對方你想請某人來聽電話，英語的說法就是用這個「Can I...?」的句型，中文意思是「我想跟某人說話，行嗎？」，其實是在跟對方說「我打電話來是想找某人說話」，或是「請你叫某人來聽電話」。

Could I leave a message?

打電話時，「留話」的英語就是 leave a message，如

果你想要留話，英語的說法就是用上一個「Could I...?」的句型，問「我可以留話嗎？」，這句話表面上是請求對方的同意，讓你留話，實際上是跟對方說「我想留話」，說法就是 Could I leave a message?

Could I take a message?

跟上一句話相反的情形是，對方打電話來要找某人，而那個人正好不在，或是他正忙沒時間聽電話，你問對方要不要留話，這種情形同樣是用「Could I...?」的句型問「我可以接下你的留話（take a message)嗎？」，實際上你是問對方「要不要留話」。

Could I tell Mary who's calling?

當有人打電話來要找瑪麗聽電話，你要問他是誰，好跟瑪麗說是誰要找她，同樣是用「Could I...?」這個句型問「我可以跟瑪麗說是誰打來的嗎？」，英語就是 Could I tell Mary who's calling?

Could I have her call you?

如果有人打電話來，要找某人聽電話，而這個人不在，或是他正在忙，沒時間聽電話，你除了問對方要不要留話之外，也可以問對方「你需要她回你電話嗎？／我請她回你電話，好嗎？」，英語的說法就是 Could I have her call you?

●問對方是否要留言，可以這麼問。

[M] Is Mary there?

[W] She's out shopping right now.

Could I take a message?

[M] 瑪麗在嗎？
[W] 她出去購物了。
　　你要留話嗎？

●表達再回電話給對方，就這麼說。

[M] John's busy right now.
Could I have him call you?

[W] That would be great.

My name's Mary, and he should have my number.

[M] 約翰現在正忙著。
　　我請他再打給你好嗎？
[W] 很好。
　　我叫瑪麗，他應該有我的電話號碼。

●問人家是否要留言，也可以這麼說。

[W] Can I speak to Mr. Lin?

[M] He just stepped out of the office.

May I take a message?

[W] No, thank you.

I'll call back later.

[W] 請林先生聽電話。
[M] 他正好剛離開辦公室。
你要留話嗎？

[W] 不用，謝謝你。
我稍後再打。

快熟句型---記住真好用

- Can I speak to Mary?
  請瑪麗聽電話。

- Could I leave a message?
  我可以留話嗎？

- Could I take a message?
  你要留話嗎？

- Could I tell Mary who's calling?
  請問你是誰？（我可以跟瑪麗說是誰打來的嗎？）

- Could I have him call you?
  我請他打給你好嗎？

message	['mɛsɪdʒ]	（名）留言；訊息
busy	['bɪzɪ]	（形）忙的
step	[stɛp]	（動）跨步；行走；前進
later	['letɚ]	（副）稍後

22. Could I call you later?

我稍後再打給你，好嗎？

Could I call you back later?

文法句型解說

Can I...

前面提過請求對方同意的英語有三種句型；「May I + 你要對方同意的事？」，「Can I + 你要對方同意的事？」，和「Could I + 你要對方同意的事？」，例如：你媽媽正要出門，你想跟她一起去，你就可以問她說 May I come with you? 或 Can I come with you? 或 Could I come with you?

call you later

call 當動詞，可以做「打電話」的意思，如果你要告訴對方「我稍後再打電話給你」，就是 I'll call you later. 如果你因現在正忙，沒有時間跟對方說話，你向對方說

「我稍後再打電話給你好嗎？」，套進上面的句型就是：
Can I call you later? 或Could I call you later? 或
May I call you later?

Could you hold?

「Can I + 你要對方同意的事？」是想請求對方同意的
句型，如果你想「請對方做某件事」，就要用「Can you
+ 你要對方同意的事？」，或「Could you + 你要對方
同意的事？」這兩個句型。
如果有人打電話來，你要對方「電話拿著稍候」，要
用 hold 這個字，英語的說法就是 Can you hold? 或
Could you hold?。記住：在電話中要對方稍待一下，是
用hold這個字，而不是用 wait。

說得漂亮--實況會話

●再打電話聯絡，就這麼說。

[W] I've really enjoyed this conversation.

[M] Me, too.
Could I call you later, and we could go
grab a pizza or something?

[W] Sure, I'm looking forward to it.

[W] 跟你聊天真的很愉快。
[M] 我也是。
我以後可以打電話給你，我們一起去吃個披薩
餅，或是其他什麼嗎？

W 好啊，我會等你的電話。

●等會兒再回電，可以這樣說。

M Hi Mary.
This is John.

W How are you, John?
Could I call you back later?
I'in the middle of something right now.

M No problem.

M 嗨，瑪麗。
我是約翰。

W 約翰，你好嗎？
我待會兒再打給你好嗎？
我現在正忙著。

M 好，沒問題。

●要電話中的人等一下，這麼說最簡單。

W Is Mr. Lin there?

M Could you hold?

W 林先生在嗎？

M 請你稍候一下好嗎？

Tip !---英語小知識

Who are you holding for?

「拿著電話、別掛斷、稍等一下」的英語是「hold」，

如果你看到電話沒掛著，你知道電話那一端有人等著，你要問對方「你在等著跟誰說電話？」，英語的說法就是 Who are you holding for?

●要電話中的人等一下，這麼說顯得很有禮貌。

[W] IBM customer service.

Could you hold on one moment?

[M] Yes.

[W] Be right with you.

> [W] IBM公司的顧客服務部。
> 請你稍候一下好嗎？
>
> [M] 好的。
>
> [W] 我馬上就來。

快熟句型---記住真好用

- May I ask who's calling?
  請問你是誰？

- May I ask who this is?
  請問你是誰？

- Could I call you back later?
  我稍後再打給你好嗎？

- I'm in the middle of something.
  我正在做別的事情。

- I'm on another line.

  我正在講另一支電話。

超實用單字---1秒就記住

really [ˈrilɪ]	（副）真的
enjoy [ɪnˈdʒɔɪ]	（動）喜歡；感到樂趣
conversation [ˌkɑnvɚˈseʃən]	（名）談話
grab [græb]	（動）匆忙地拿；隨便吃一下
pizza [ˈpɪzə]	（名）披薩餅
middle [ˈmɪdl̩]	（名）中間
hold [hold]	（動）（電話）稍待
customer [ˈkʌstəmɚ]	（名）顧客
service [ˈsɝvɪs]	（名）服務
another [əˈnʌðɚ]	（形）另一個的
line [laɪn]	（名）電話線

23. Can I use your rest room?

我可以借用你們的洗手間嗎？

Can I use your rest room?

文法句型解說

Can I...?

「Can I...?」這個句型，表面上是在「請求對方的同意」，實際上也含有跟對方說「我想要這麼做」的意思。

如果你要問對方「洗手間在哪裡？」，或是告訴對方「我想使用你們的洗手間，請問洗手間在哪裡」，洗手間的英文，在公共場所是說 rest room，如果是在別人家裡，則是說 bathroom。

如果你在公共場所，想使用洗手間，就要說 Can I use your rest room? 或 Could I use your rest room? 或 May I use your rest room?

如果是在朋友家裡，你就可以說 Can I use your bathroom? 或 Could I use your bathroom? 或 May I use your bathroom?

說得漂亮--實況會話

●要借用洗手間，要學會說得有禮貌。

[W] Can I use your rest room?

I'd like to freshen up.

[M] Right this way, ma'am.

[W] 我可以借用你們的洗手間嗎？
我需要梳洗一下。

[M] 小姐，洗手間往這裡走。

●問洗手間怎麼走就是這樣問。

[W] Which way to the rest room, sir?

[M] Just follow me.

[W] 先生，洗手間往哪裡走？
[M] 請跟我來。

快熟句型---記住真好用

- Can I use your rest room?
  我可以借用你們的洗手間嗎？

- ● Can I use your bathroom?
  我可以借用你們的洗手間嗎？

use [juz]	（動）使用
freshen [ˈfrɛʃən]	（動）梳洗；使恢復精神
follow [ˈfɑlo]	（動）跟隨
way [we]	（名）路程；方向

24. Would you please?
那就麻煩你了。

Would you please?

文法句型解說

Would you please?

當有人提議幫你做某件事時，若是你要讓他幫你做，你可以回答 Yes, please. 或者你也可以回答 Would you please?。這句話是很道地、很有禮貌的英語，按照字面翻譯是「可以請你這麼做嗎？」，實際上對方已經提議要幫你做了，所以這句話的意思是「那就麻煩你了。」

Can I take your coat?

take可以做「把某樣東西拿到某個地方去」的意思，例如：有人到你家來作客，你通常都會等客人把外衣或圍巾脫下來後，再把衣物拿去放好，英語的說法就是，

Can I take your coat and scarf?

你要我幫你拿外套和圍巾去放嗎？

●人家要幫忙，這樣回答就對了。

[W] Do you want me to take this over to the post office?

[M] Would you please?

　[W] 你要我把這個拿到郵局嗎？
　[M] 那就麻煩你了。

●「麻煩你。」英文這麼說。

[W] Can I take your coat?

[M] Would you please?

　[W] 你要我幫你拿外套去放嗎？
　[M] 那就麻煩你了。

快熟句型---記住真好用

- Would you please?
  那就麻煩你了。

- Can I take your coat?
  你要我幫你拿外套去放嗎？

- Can you take me to the airport tomorrow?

你明天可以帶我去機場嗎？

- Take this form to Mr. Lin, ask him to sign it, and then bring it back.

  把這張表格拿去給林先生，請他簽名，然後再拿回來。

超實用單字---1秒就記住

post office	郵局
sign [saɪn]	（動）簽名
back [bæk]	（副）回來
form [fɔrm]	（名）表格
airport [ˈɛrˌport]	（名）飛機場
coat [kot]	（名）大衣；外套

What are your hours?

文法句型解說

What are your hours?

商店營業的時間，或是公司有人在上班的時間，英語是 hours，所以如果你要問某家商店營業的時間，英語的說法就是 What are your hours? 或 Can you tell me your hours?

這兩句話的問法是在問一般營業的時間，所以當你這麼問一家商店的店員時，他們通常會回答你「他們每天是從幾點開到幾點」，例如：他們若是從早上十點開到下午七點，英語的說法就是 We're open from 10:00 to 7:00.

What are your hours today?

What are your hours today? 是問商店今天營業的時間

是什麼時候，店家可能會回答你 We opened at 8:00. And we close at 10:00. （我們今天是八點開門的，十點打烊。）由於你問的時候，他們應該已經開門在營業了，所以會用「過去式動詞opened」，但是他們打烊的時間還沒到，所以會用「現在簡單式動詞close」。

當然，店家不一定會回答說他們是幾點開門，然後幾點關門，他們也可能回答你 We're open from 10:00 to 7:00 today.

The bank is open until 3:00.

open 也可以當形容詞，意思是「營業中」，我們若是要說這家銀行都是開到三點，可以用形容詞 open，因為 open 是形容詞，所以 open 的前面要有個「be 動詞，are 或 is」，。這裡的主詞是 the bank，所以要用 is，整句英語的說法是 The bank is open until 3:00. 你也可以說這家銀行是三點關門，英語的說法是 The bank closes at 3:00.

Are you open this weekend?

若你想問某家商店週末有沒有開，正確的說法是 Are you open this weekend? 若是他們週末有營業，你可能聽到這樣的回答：

Yes, we're open until 2:00 p.m. on both days.

有，週末那兩天我們都是開到兩點。

若是他們沒有營業，他們會回答你：

No, we're closed. 或是 No, we are not open.

closed是個形容詞，它的用法在下一單元，會有詳細的說明。

What time do you open?

open 當動詞時，是「開始營業」的意思，所以若你不是要問商店營業的時間，而是想問他們「每天幾點開始營業」，可以用「動詞open」來問，英語的說法是：
What time do you open? （或 When do you open?）
而對方可能回答你 We open at 8:00.
注意：這裡說的是通常每天開始營業的時間，要用現在簡單式動詞 open.

說得漂亮--實況會話

● 問營業時間的一種說法。

W　What are your hours?

M　We're open from 10:00 to 7:00.

　　W 請問你們營業時間是從幾點到幾點？
　　M 我們從十點開到七點。

● 問營業時間的另一種說法。

W　What are your hours **today**?

M　We opened at 9:00 and we close at 10:00 tonight.

　　W 今天你們的營業時間是幾點到幾點？
　　M 我們九點開門，晚上十點打烊。

●問商家明天有開嗎，很簡單。

[W] Are you open tomorrow?

[M] No, we are not open tomorrow.

[W] 你們明天有開嗎？
[M] 沒有，我們明天不營業。

●24小時營業的說法怎麼說？

[W] Would you tell me what your hours are today?

[M] We're open 24 hours a day.

[W] 請問你們今天的營業時間是從幾點到幾點？
[M] 我們一天二十四小時都開。

●問幾點開門，怎麼問？

[W] When do you open?

[M] We open at 9:00.

[W] 你們幾點開始營業？
[M] 我們九點開門。

●詢問店是否有開，就這麼問。

[W] ABC Department Store.

[M] Hello, I just wanted to find out if you were open today.

[W] Yes, we are.

Our weekend hours are the same as weekdays, 9:00 a.m. to 9:00 p.m.

Ⓦ 這裡是ABC 貨公司。

Ⓜ 哈囉，我只是想知道你們今天有沒有營業。

Ⓦ 有，我們今天有開。
我們週末營業時間跟週日一樣，上午九點到晚上九點。

快熟句型---記住真好用

- What are your hours?
  請問你們營業時間是從幾點到幾點？

- Can you tell me your hours?
  請問你們營業時間是從幾點到幾點？

- The bank is open until 3:00.
  銀行開到三點。

- Are you open this weekend?
  這個週末你們有營業嗎？

- We're open from 10:00 to 7:00.
  我們的營業時間是從十點到七點。

- We're open 24 hours a day.
  我們一天二十四小時都開。

- When do you open?
  你們幾點開始營業？

- We open at 9:00.
  我們九點開始營業。

超實用單字---1秒就記住

weekend [ˈwikˈɛnd]	（名）週末
same [sem]	（形）相同的
weekday [ˈwikˌde]	（名）平日（星期一到星期五）
open [ˈopən]	（動）開門；開始營業 （形）開著；有營業的

Can you tell me when you close?

文法句型解說

closed

上一單元提過，closed 當形容詞是指「沒有營業」的意思，是 open 的相反詞，所以若是有人問你們週末有沒有營業，若是沒有，你就可以回答說：We are not open on weekends. 或是 We are closed on weekends.

The shop is closed on Sundays.

若是我們要說這家商店星期天都沒有營業，可以用形容詞 closed （沒有營業）或 open （營業中）來說，整句英語的說法是 The shop is closed on Sundays. 或是 The shop is not open on Sundays.

close

close 是動詞，是「商店打烊」的意思。若是你想知道某家商店幾點打烊，你就可以說：What time do you close? 或 When do you close?

說得漂亮--實況會話

●不營業，怎麼說？

W Are you open this weekend?

M No, we're closed.

> W 這個週末你們有營業嗎？
> M 沒有，這個週末我們不營業。

●不開放，怎麼說？

W Let's go visit the Botanic Garden.

M The garden is closed to visitors in winter.

> W 我們到植物園去玩。
> M 植物園冬天不對外開放。

●問開放時間，就這麼問。

W What are your hours today?

M We opened at 9:00 and we close at 10:00 tonight.

> W 你們今天從幾點開到幾點？
> M 我們九點開門，今晚十點打烊。

W　Can you tell me when you close?

M　We close at 8:00.

　　W 請問你們幾點打烊？
　　M 我們八點打烊。

Tip !---英語小知識

Can you tell me...

當你想請問對方，告訴你一些你想知道的答案，英語的基本句型就是「Can you tell me + 你想要對方告訴你的？」，例如：你想知道對方的商店幾點關門，英語是 Can you tell me when you close?

又如：你想請對方告訴你，到火車站怎麼走，英語的說法是 Can you tell me how to get to the train station?

快熟句型---記住真好用

- What are you doing this weekend?
  這個週末你要做什麼？

- Are you doing anything this weekend?
  你這個週末有什麼事嗎？

- I never work on weekends.
  我週末不上班。

- Can you tell me your hours?

  你們的營業時間是從幾點到幾點？

- Can you tell me when you close?

  請問你們什麼時候打烊？

- Can you tell me where the Central library is?

  請問中央圖書館在哪裡？

closed [klozd]	（形）沒有營業的
close [kloz]	（動）（商店）打烊
visit ['vɪzɪt]	（動）訪問；拜訪
botanic [bo'tænɪk]	（形）植物的
garden ['gɑrdn̩]	（名）花園
visitor ['vɪzɪtɚ]	（動）訪客
winter ['wɪntɚ]	（名）冬天

I'll trade you.

I'll trade you...

當你想拿你的某樣東西跟對方交換他的某樣東西時，英語的句型是：「I'll trade you 我的某樣東西 for 你的某樣東西」，例如：你想用你的手錶去換對方的手鐲時，英語的說法就是：I'll trade you this watch for your bracelet. 如果要與對方換同樣物品，那只要說 yours（你的那個）就可以了，完整的句子是 I'll trade you this watch for yours.

trade something in

當你要買一部新車時，你拿你的舊車子給車行，折合一些錢來抵一部分買新車的錢，英語的說法是「trade 這

部舊車 in for 另一部新車」，或 「trade 這部舊車 in on 另一部新車」。

●以物易物，怎麼說？

M I'll trade you my genuine leather jacket for your mink coat.

W It's a deal.

I like leather better anyway.

M 我用我的真皮夾克，換你的貂皮大衣。
W 就這麼説定了。
我反正較喜歡皮製的。

●要和對方交換某物，可以這麼說。

W I have a peanut butter sandwich today.

M I'll trade you.

I have a hamburger.

W 我今天帶了花生醬三明治。
M 我跟你換。
我有漢堡。

●問人用什麼東西來換，這麼說。

W What will you trade for the bugle?

What about your old flute?

> Ⓦ 你要我用什麼東西來換你的喇叭？
> Ⓜ 用你的舊長笛來換，好嗎？

●同意某個交易，這麼說就表示談定了。

Ⓦ OK. $500, but that's my last offer.

Ⓜ OK, it's a deal.

> Ⓦ 好，五塊錢，這可是我的底價了。
> Ⓜ 好，就這麼說定了。

Tip !---英語小知識

It's a deal.

當你在跟人商討一件事情，或是你在跟對方商討買賣條件，當你覺得對方說到一個你可以接受的條件時，你就可以說 It's a deal.（好，就這麼說定了。）

快熟句型---記住真好用

● John turned down our offer of $2000 for his old car.
約翰拒絕我們要用兩千塊錢買他的舊車的提議。

● The two teams did a deal and John was traded.
兩支隊伍談妥了條件，約翰就被換到另一支隊伍去了。

● I traded my old car in for a new one.
我拿我的舊車折合一些價錢，買了一部新車。

trade [tred]	（動）貿易；交換
genuine [ˈdʒɛnjʊɪn]	（形）純正的
leather [ˈlɛðɚ]	（名）皮革
jacket [ˈdʒækɪt]	（名）夾克；外套
mink [mɪŋk]	（名）貂皮
coat [kot]	（名）大衣；外套
sandwich [ˈsændwɪtʃ]	（名）三明治
hamburger [ˈhæmbɚgɚ]	（名）漢堡
bugle [ˈbjugl̩]	（名）喇叭
flute [flut]	（名）長笛
offer [ˈɔfɚ]	（名）（價格～）提議
deal [dil]	（名）交易
team [tim]	（名）隊伍；團隊

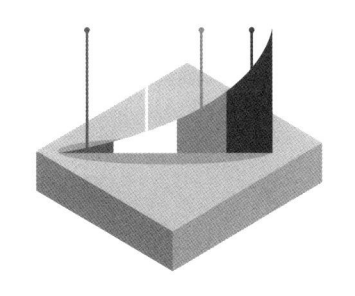

My treat.

文法句型解說

My treat.

treat 做「請客」的意思時，也可以當名詞。如果你約對方去吃東西，或一起去看電影，而你想請客，就可以說 my treat（我請客。）例如：

Let's go to the movies, my treat.

我們去看電影，我請客。

my treat 這句話也可以用在大家吃完飯、準備結帳付款時，你把帳單拿過來，說 my treat，表示你要請客。

如果有人請客，你要謝謝對方，你就可以說 Thanks for the treat.

I'll treat you to a pizza.

treat 當動詞時，可以當「請客」的意思。若你想請別人吃什麼東西，句型就是「I'll treat you to + 你要請對方吃的東西」，例如：你想請對方吃冰淇淋，你就可以跟他說：

I'll treat you to some ice cream.
我請你吃冰淇淋。

The treat is on me.

The treat is on me. 這句話的用法跟 My treat. 一樣，不論是請大家去吃飯，或是大家吃完飯，準備結帳付款時，你把帳單拿過來說要請客，都可以用這句話。如：

Let's go to "Seafood King" for dinner. The treat is on me.
我們到「海鮮大王」去吃晚飯，我請客。

The treat is on me. 也可以換成 It's on me.

I'm buying.

I'm buying. 也是「我請客」的意思，它的用法跟 The treat is on me. 和 my treat 都一樣。

Let me buy you a drink.

當你有事情跟對方談，或是想要坐下來大家聊聊天時，你就可以說 Let me buy you a drink. 意思就是「我請你去喝杯飲料。」

pick up the bill.

bill 這個字是「帳單」的意思，大家一起去吃飯，誰pick up the bill，就是他要付錢請吃飯的意思。

Let's each pay our own way.

「大家各付各的」英語，一般人學的說法都是「Go Dutch.」，這是比較老式的說法，美國人較常說的是 Let's each pay our own way.

說得漂亮--實況會話

●要請客，兩個字OK。

W Come on.

Let's go out for some ice cream, my treat.

M Thanks.

I owe you one.

W 來吧。

我請你去吃冰淇淋。

M 謝了。

我就欠你一次。

●要請人家喝東西，說起來就是這麼簡單。

W That was a great movie.

Come on. Let me buy you a drink.

M No thanks.

It's late. I think I should head on home.

W 那部電影真棒。

來吧，我請你喝杯飲料。

Ⓜ 不用了，謝謝。

很晚了。我想我該回家了。

●要請客，還可以這樣說。

Ⓦ It's Mary's Birthday.

Let's all go out to eat in celebration.
I'm buying.

Ⓜ Sounds like a great idea.

Where do you have in mind?

Ⓦ 今天是瑪麗的生日。

我們一起到外面吃飯慶祝。

我請客。

Ⓜ 聽起來不錯。

你想去哪裡？

快熟句型---記住真好用

- Could I buy you a drink?
  我請你喝杯飲料好嗎？

- Let's all go out to eat. I'm buying.
  我們都到外面餐廳去吃飯，我請客。

- Why don't you all join me at the Chili?
  你們何不都跟我到「奇麗餐廳」去？

I'll treat everyone to steaks.

我請大家去吃牛排。

● You'd better come with us.

你最好跟我們一起來。

John is going to treat us all to dessert at May's.

約翰要請我們大家一起去「小美冰店」吃點心。

快熟句型---記住真好用

● I'm starving. How about a burger and fries, my treat?

我餓死了。我們去吃漢堡和薯條，好嗎？我請客。

Tip !---英語小知識

How about...?

How about...? 這句話是用在大家在商討一個方法，或是要去哪裡，或是商討時間，或是商討要做什麼事，你要提出建議時，例如：大家在商討什麼時候開會，你建議「星期五」，英語的說法就是 How about Friday?

超實用單字---1秒就記住

treat [trit]	（名）請客（動）請客
owe [o]	（動）虧欠

drink [drɪŋk]	（名）飲料	
celebration [ˌsɛləˈbreʃən]	（名）慶祝	
mind [maɪnd]	（名）頭腦	
idea [aɪˈdiə]	（名）主意	
keen [kin]	（形）熱衷的	
steak [stek]	（名）牛排	
dessert [dɪˈzɝt]	（名）（飯後）甜點	
starving [ˈstɑrvɪŋ]	（形）很餓	
burger [ˈbɝɡɚ]	（名）漢堡	
fries [fraɪz]	（名）薯條	

29. Now you're talking!
你這麼說才像話。

Now you are talking.

文法句型解說

Now you're talking!

當你認為對方說出了你認為他應該說的話，或是對方說的話是你愛聽的話，你就可以跟他說 Now you're talking!

Look who's talking!

當有人指責你某件事做得不對，而你不服對方的指責，因為你認為對方在他指責你的事情上面也是跟你半斤八兩，你就可以回他一句 Look who's talking!。例如：你的姊姊總是把熱門音樂放得很大聲，對於這一點，你一直很受不了，有一天，當你在聽音樂時，她來指責你音樂放得太大聲，吵到她讀書，你若是願意接受她的指

責，把音樂關小聲一點就算了，如果你覺得她自己也是如此，你不接受她的指責時，你就可以回她一句 Look who's talking!

●別人說了中聽的話，這樣表達最恰當。

[W] What's going on this weekend?

[M] Nothing so far.

[W] Well, in that case, I think I'll throw a party at my house.

[M] Now you are talking.

[W] 這個週末有什麼節目？
M: 到目前為止，還沒有什麼計畫。

[W] 那，這樣的話， 我想在我家開個宴會。
[M] 你說這一句話最中聽。

Tip !---英語小知識

in that case

in that case是個片語，意思是「那樣的話」、「如果情形是這樣的話」。

throw a party

當你想舉辦一個宴會時，你可以說 I'm going to throw a party.

舉辦一個宴會，動詞用throw這個字，看起來好像很奇

怪，但這是很常見又道地的説法，學起來就對了。

●贊同別人說的話，這樣說就對了。

W I won't put up with her behavior any more.

I'll tell her exactly what I think of it.

M Now you're talking.

W 我不能再縱容她的行為了。
我要告訴她，我對她行為的看法。

M 你説這句話才像話。

●不贊同別人說的話，可以這樣隱喻。

W You know.

It's not polite to ignore people you dis-like.

M Look who's talking!

I never see you talking to Julie or Mike either.

W 你知道嗎！
你不喜歡的人，你就不理他，那是不禮貌的。

M 唉呀，烏鴉笑豬黑！
我從來沒看過你跟 莉或邁可説過話。

- Now you're talking!
  你說這一句話最中聽。

- Look who's talking.
  唉呀，烏鴉笑豬黑。

- I think I'll throw a party at my house.
  我想在我家開個宴會。

throw [θro]	（動）舉辦（宴會）
behavior [bɪ'hevjɚ]	（名）規矩；行為
exactly [ɪg'zæktlɪ]	（副）確切地
polite [pə'laɪt]	（形）禮貌的；客氣的
dislike [dɪs'laɪk]	（動）不喜歡

Well, look who's here.

文法句型解說

Look who's here!

當你說 Look who's here! 時，就是叫另外一個人注意，這裡有一個人，你來看看是誰。這句話通常用在你不期而遇的老朋友，或是見到你不想見到的人。

有時你帶了老朋友回家，你叫你的家人來看看你帶了誰回來時，你也可以說 Look who's here!

Look,...

有時在你開口說話之前，先說聲「Look,」再繼續你要說的話，這只是含有叫對方一聲的意思而已，並沒有要對方真的看什麼的意思。

Look at that!

Look at that! 的用法跟 Look, 的用法不一樣，Look at that! 這句話真的是叫對方看看某件事情，例如：你到餐廳吃飯，結果你發現比你晚到的人已經上菜了，而你們這桌卻還沒有上菜，你就可以跟你同桌的人說 Look at that!，意思就是那桌的人比我們晚到，為什麼他們的菜已經來了。

說得漂亮--實況會話

●某人的到來讓你很驚訝時，就這麼說。

M　Mary, look who's here for dinner.

W　Why, John!

I haven't seen you in years.

You haven't changed one bit.

M 瑪麗，你看是誰來我們家吃晚飯。

W 什麼，是約翰。

我好久沒看到你了。

你一點都沒變。

●和老朋友不期而遇，這樣表達最恰當。

W　Hi, John.

M　Well, look who's here.

You've been keeping busy these past few months, Mary.

W 嗨，約翰。

M 嘿，我還以為是誰呢。

瑪麗，你過去幾個月可真忙啊。

- Look who's here! It's John and Mary.
  看看誰來了。是約翰和瑪麗呢！

- Look, why don't you think about it and give me your answer tomorrow?
  嘿，你何不想想看，明天再告訴我你要怎麼做？

- Look at that!
  你看看。

  Those people came in after we did and they're being served already.
  那些人比我們晚進來，已經有人在服務他們了。

change [tʃendʒ]	（動）改變	
busy [ˈbɪzɪ]	（形）忙的	
answer [ˈænsɚ]	（名）答案；回答	
serve [sɝv]	（動）上菜；服務	

Did you hear that sound?

文法句型解說

I'll go look.

大家學過,在動詞後面如果要接另一個動詞,要接to,再接另一個動詞,但是在英語會話中,若說要去做某件事,常用 go,後面直接跟著要去做的動詞,例如:瑪麗跟你說,外面好像有什麼奇怪的聲音,你說你會去看看,英語口語的說法是 I'll go look.

go see a movie

go後面直接跟著要去做的動詞還有許多,例如:go see a movie(去看電影)。如果你想問對方今晚要不要去看電影,整句話就是 Would you like to go see a movie tonight?

go get something

go get something（去拿點東西）也是同樣的用法，例如：「我清理客廳之後，要去拿點東西吃」，英語就是 I'm going to clean up the living room and then go get something to eat.

●想邀請別人看電影，可以這樣問。

[W] You've done a great job with this lawsuit.

[M] Thank you.
I couldn't have pulled it off without your help.

[W] Well, since that's over with, do you want to go see a movie tomorrow night?

[M] That sounds like a great idea.

[W] 這個訴訟事件你做得很好。
[M] 謝謝你。
沒有你的幫忙，我做不成的。
[W] 嗯，既然事情已經過去了，明晚你要不要去看部電影？
[M] 聽起來是個好主意。

pull something off

pull something off 是一個片語，意思是「把某件事情做成功」。例如：你知道約翰希望能考上台大，你跟瑪麗說我希望他考得上，英語的說法是 I hope he can pull it off.

● 到處看看、巡視，可以這樣說。

W　John? Did you hear that sound?

M　No, but I'll go look around anyway.

W 約翰，你有沒有聽到什麼聲音？
M 沒有，但是我還是到處看看好了。

快熟句型---記住真好用

- I'll go look.
  我會去看看。

- What do you say we go get a bite to eat?
  我們去吃個東西，你看怎麼樣？

- Would you like to go see a movie tonight?
  你今晚要去看電影嗎？

lawsuit [ˈlɔˌsut]	（名）訴訟
since [sɪns]	（連）自從
sound [saʊnd]	（名）聲音
anyway [ˈɛnɪˌwe]	（副）無論如何
bite [baɪt]	（名）一口；簡單的飲食

32. I'll see what I can do.
我盡量試試看。

I'll see what I can do.

文法句型解說

I'll see what I can do.

當你請美國人幫你忙時，除非這件事情是小事一樁，他很有把握可以做得成，否則他通常不會回答「Yes, Sure, Certainly」等很肯定的話，即使他願意幫忙，他也會回答你說 I'll see what I can do.

I'll see what I can do. 照字面的意思就是「我看看我能做什麼」，也就是他雖然答應幫忙，但是他只能盡力而為，他不跟你保證他一定能做得成。

●告訴別人我會盡力而為，就這麼說。

[W] John, my washing machine has broken down for the fifth time this month.

[M] I'll be right over.

I'll see what I can do.

[W] 約翰，我的洗衣機這個月已經是第五次壞了。
[M] 我馬上過來。
我看看我能不能幫你修理。

Tip !---英語小知識

break down

break down 這個片語當動詞是「機器壞了」的意思，它的形容詞「壞的」，英語是 broken-down；break-down 是「名詞」，「壞掉」的意思。

●告訴別人你會處理，你會安排，就這麼說。

[W] It's our honeymoon.

And I'd like to sit where we can have a great view of the falls.

[M] I'll see to it.

[W] 我們在度蜜月。
我想要一個我們可以好好欣賞瀑布的桌位。
[M] 我來盡量安排看看。

I'll see to it.

see to it 是個片語，意思是「照料一下」、「處理一下」。若遇到事情需要處理或安排，如：「我會處理」或是「我會安排」，英語的説法是 I'll see to it.

快熟句型---記住真好用

- I'll see what I can do.
  我盡量試試看。

- Let's see.
  我們來看看。

- I'll see to it.
  我來安排看看。

- I hear the doorbell.
  我聽到門鈴聲。

- Will someone please see to it?
  誰有空去應門？

- This form needs filling out.
  這張表格需要填寫。

  Will you see to it?
  你填一下好嗎？

- The car broke down in the middle of the highway.

  車子在高速公路途中拋錨了。

- Get this broken-down lawn mower out of here!

  把這個壞了的割草機拿出去。

- This car has had one breakdown after another.

  這部車子一壞再壞。

owe [o]		（動）虧欠
honeymoon [ˈhʌnɪˌmun]		（名）蜜月
view [vju]		（名）景觀；風景
doorbell [ˈdorˌbɛl]		（名）門鈴
form [fɔrm]		（名）表格
middle [ˈmɪdl̩]		（名）中間
highway [ˈhaɪwe]		（名）高速公路
lawn mower		割草機
breakdown [ˈbrekˌdaʊn]		（名）壞了

33. How's it going?
你好嗎？

How are you doing?

How's it going?

兩個人見了面打招呼，基本上是彼此問好，問好的內容有很多種，你可以問「你好嗎？」，或是「你最近做的事情順利嗎？」，或是「最近你有什麼事嗎？」，如果很久沒見面，就問「你這一陣子好嗎？」實際上，英語的招呼語很多，How are you? 是最基本的說法，但美國人見面打招呼，並不是一成不變說 How are you? 而已，在這麼多打招呼英語中，到底在哪種情況下要用哪一個呢？其實，只要瞭解這些招呼語真正在說什麼，自然就清楚到底什麼時候該用哪句話了。

從 How's it going? 這句話，你可以看得出是在問「事情進行的怎麼樣？」，問這句話時，你不一定特定問哪一件對方在做的事情，只是概括性地問對方「一切順利

155

嗎」的意思，所以，當你見到朋友，你想問他「你最近做的事情順利嗎」，就可以用 How's it going? 來打招呼。

How are you?

How are you? 問的是最廣泛的「你好嗎？」，一般不管對於不熟的人或是熟朋友，都可以用這句話來打招呼。

How are you doing?

How are you doing? 這句話跟 How are you? 的用法比較接近。How are you? 是問對方「你好嗎？」，How are you doing? 照字面的意思是「你做得好嗎？」，兩句話都是很通常的招呼語。

I'm doing okay.

當有人用 How are you doing? 這句話來跟你打招呼時，你可以回答 I'm doing fine. 或 I'm doing okay.

How have you been?

當你遇到一個許久未見的朋友時，你可能會想問他「這一陣子好嗎？」，那麼就用 How have you been? 這句話來打招呼。

What's up?

What's up? 的意思是「有什麼新鮮事？」「有什麼好玩的？」，在這個單元裡，這句話就是問「有什麼新鮮事」的意思。

What's up? 也常用在兩個很熟的朋友見面時，打招呼的話。其實兩個朋友見了面，說這句話的本意還是在問對

方「近來有什麼事？」，在熟朋友間，彼此不想文謅謅地問 How are you? 所以就問 What's up?

問對方「近來有什麼事嗎」的招呼語，除了 What's up? 之外，還有 What's new? 和 What's happening? 等等說法。

說得漂亮--實況會話

●有精神的打招呼方式。

M Hi, Mary. How's it going?

W Oh, hi, John.

Not too well, I'm afraid.

M Why? What's the matter?

W I've got a splitting headache.

That's all.

M 嗨，瑪麗。你好嗎？

W 噢，嗨，約翰。

我恐怕不太好。

M 怎麼啦？

W 我的頭很痛。

就是這樣。

●最普通的打招呼方式。

W How are you?

M　Fine, thanks. And you?

　　W　你好嗎？
　　M　很好，謝謝，你呢？

●關心的打招呼方式。

W　How have you been?

M　**Pretty good.**

　　W　你近來好嗎？
　　M　很好。

●問人家有事嗎，也是打招呼的方式。

W　What's happening?

M　**Not much.**

　　W　有什麼事嗎？
　　M　沒什麼？

●問有什麼新鮮事的打招呼方式。

W　What's new?

M　**Nothing.**

　　W　近來可有什麼變？
　　M　沒什麼。

●十分常用的打招呼方式。

W　How are you doing?

M I'm doing okay. And you?

W 你好嗎？
M 還好，你呢？

快熟句型---記住真好用

- How's it going?
  一切還好嗎？

- How are you?
  你好嗎？

- How have you been?
  你這一陣子可好？

- How are you doing?
  你好嗎？

- What's new?
  最近有什麼事嗎？

- What's up?
  最近有什麼事嗎？

- What's happening?
  最近有什麼事發生嗎？

- I'm doing okay.
  我還好。

afraid [əˈfred]	（形）恐怕	
matter [ˈmætɚ]	（What's ）事情	
splitting [ˈsplɪtɪŋ]	（形）劇痛的；爆裂似的	
headache [ˈhɛdˌek]	（What's ）頭痛	
pretty [ˈprɪtɪ]	（副）非常；相當	
happening [ˈhæpənɪŋ]	（動）發生（happen的現在分詞）	

I've been there.

文法句型解說

I've been there.

I've been there. 這句話很有用，按照字面的翻譯是「我曾經到過那裡」的意思。在美語會話中，當有人跟你說一件他所經歷的不愉快的事情時，你若是要跟他說「我瞭解你在說什麼」，或是「我瞭解你的感受」，因為我也經歷過，那就要說 I've been there.，對方聽了一定會很感動你的體貼！

說得漂亮--實況會話

●和別人有感同身受的說法。

W　Those board meetings really wear me out.

M I know what you mean.

I've been there.

W: 那些董事會議真使我累慘了。

M 我知道你的意思。

我也曾經歷過。

wear 某人out

wear當動詞，用作片語「wear 某人 out」時，意思是「把某人累壞了」，或是「把某人累慘了」。wear 的過去式是 wore，過去分詞是worn。

●有同樣經驗，也可以這樣說。

W May I borrow your phone to call a locksmith?

I locked myself out of the car.

M Sure, the phone is over there.

I've been there.

W 我可以借用你的電話打個電話給鎖匠嗎？

我把鑰匙鎖在車子裡。

M 請用，電話就在那裡。

我也曾經把鑰匙鎖在車子裡。

快熟句型---記住真好用

• I've been there.

我也曾經歷過。

- Two nights without sleep have worn me out.
  兩個晚上沒有睡覺把我累壞了。

- You look worn out!
  你看起來很累。

- Mary still keeps that pair of worn out tennis shoes.
  瑪麗還留著那一雙破舊的運 鞋。

超實用單字---1秒就記住

board [bord]	（名）委員會；董事會；理事會
meeting ['mitɪŋ]	（名）會議
mean [min]	（動）意思是
locksmith ['lɑk͵smɪθ]	（名）鎖匠
tennis shoes	運動鞋
pair [pɛr]	（名）一雙

35. That depends.
那要看是什麼情況了。

MP3-36

That depends.

文法句型解說

That depends.

當有人對你提出要求時，有時候你不會一下子就答應，
因為你得先聽聽詳情再說，所以你就可以回答對方說
That depends.，意思就是「我還得先聽聽，你這個要求
有沒有其他附帶條件沒有說完」。或是有人問你將會做
某件事嗎，而你還沒有決定，因為還要看事情的發展才
能決定，你也可以回答 That depends.

It depends.

以上的情形，除了用 That depends. 之外，也可以說 It
depends.

That figures.

figure 有「瞭解」、「明白」的意思。如果某件事的發生，或某個人所做的事，是你所預期的，當有人告訴你時，你可以回答他說 That figures. 或 It figures.，表示「我就知道」的意思。

或是，你認為某件事情是合理的，或是可以理解的，你也可以說 That figures. 或 It figures.，表示「那是可以理解的」。

說得漂亮--實況會話

●看情況而定的說法。

W　Could you take care of my plants while I'm on vacation?

M　That depends.

W 我去度假的時候，你可以照顧我的花草嗎？
M 那要看情形再説。

Tip !---英語小知識

on vacation

vacation是「休假不上班」或「過節」的意思，on vacation 這個片語可以做「休假不上班」或「到外地去度假」。若是你要問對方今年要去哪裡度假，英語的説法是：

Where are you going on vacation this year?
你今年要去哪裡度假？

[M] Will you be able to come to the meeting on Friday?

[W] That depends.

[M] 你星期五可以來參加會議嗎？
[W] 我要看看我有沒有時間。

● 看情況而定的另一種說法。

[W] Are you going to Europe this summer?

[M] Well, it depends.

[W] 今年夏天你會去歐洲嗎？
[M] 嗯，看情形再說。

● 預期得到的結果。

[M] The train is behind schedule again.

[W] That figures.

[M] 火車又誤點了。
[W] 我就知道。

快熟句型---記住真好用

● That depends.
　那要看情形再說。

- That figures.

  那是可以理解的。

- Where are you going on vacation this summer?

  今年夏天你要去哪裡度假？

- I'll be away on vacation for two weeks.

  我要去度假兩星期。

- They're on vacation for the next two weeks.

  他們下兩個星期要去度假。

- Don't forget to water the plants.

  別忘了要澆花。

water the plants

美國人喜歡有各種綠色植物和花在室內，所以平常有空就得幫植物、花草澆水，英語的說法是 water the plants，注意：英語是說「water the plants」，而不是「water the flowers」，田為 plants這個字已經包括了所有的花草、植物。通常，美國人如果要出遠門，就得拜託朋友幫忙 take care of the plants，而不是 take care of the flowers。

depend [dɪ'pɛnd]	（動）視～而定；因～而定
plant [plænt]	（名）植物
vacation [ve'keʃən]	（名）休假；假期
behind [bɪ'haɪnd]	（副）在～的後面
schedule ['skɛdʒʊl]	（名）時間表
figure ['fɪgjɚ]	（動）（口語）瞭解；明白

36. I'm very dark-complexioned.

我的皮膚很黑。

You have a very nice skin tone.

文法句型解說

dark-complexioned

說一個人的「膚色黑」，是 dark-complexioned，這裡的「complexioned」是形容詞。「皮膚白」就是 light-complexioned。如果要說某個女生皮膚白／皮膚黑，英語的說法就是 She is light-complexioned / dark-complexioned.

complexion

complexion的意思是「膚色」，是名詞。當我們說某個人的皮膚很白時，可以說 She has a very light-complexion.，或是 Her complexion is rather light. （她的皮膚蠻白的。）

說得漂亮--實況會話

●膚色黑或白，怎麼說？

M　You have a very nice skin tone.

W　My mother was very dark-complexioned and my father was light.

　　I guess I got the best of both.

M 你的膚色很好。

W 我的母親膚色很黑，我的父親皮膚較白。
　　我想，我擁有雙方的優點。

●讚美人家皮膚白，這麼說。

M　Mary, you have a very light-complexion.

W　You should see me in the summer.

　　I am positively brown.

M 瑪麗，你的膚色很白。

W 你應該看看我夏天時的膚色。
　　那時，我肯定是褐色的。

●膚色相同，怎麼說？

M　Her skin tone is much lighter than Mary's.

W I actually thought they had the same skin tone.

 W 她的膚色比瑪麗的白很多。
 M 事實上，我認為她們兩個的膚色相同。

●形容淡色和深色，這麼說。

W Her hair and eyes are light brown.

And she has a dark skin color.

Now do you know who I'm talking about?

M No, I don't know who she is.

 W 她的頭髮和眼睛是淡褐色。

 而她的膚色較黑。

 那你知道我在說誰嗎？

 M 不知道，我不知道你在說誰。

快熟句型---記住真好用

- Her complexion is rather dark.
  她的膚色相當黑。

- She has a very light-complexion.
  她的膚色很白。

- She is light-complexioned.
  她的膚色白。

- John's dark-complexion comes from working in the sun.

  約翰的黑色膚色是在太陽下工作的結果。

- She had dark skin.

  她的膚色黑。

- She usually has light skin, but during the summer she gets a tan.

  她的膚色通常很白，但是夏天時，她就曬黑了。

- Her skin is very light.

  她的膚色很白。

- You must choose make-up that matches your skin tone.

  你一定要選跟你膚色相配的化妝品。

超實用單字---1秒就記住

skin [skɪn]	（名）皮膚
tone [ton]	（名）色調
complexioned [kəmˈplɛkʃənd]	（形）有～膚色的
light-complexioned	（形）膚色白的
dark-complexioned	（形）膚色黑的
complexion [kəmˈplɛkʃən]	（名）膚色

both [boθ]	（代）兩者都
dark [dɑrk]	（形）（膚色）黑的
light [laɪt]	（形）（膚色）白的
positively [ˈpɑzətɪvlɪ]	（副）肯定地
brown [braʊn]	（形）褐色的
actually [ˈæktʃʊəlɪ]	（副）實際上；事實上
thought [θɔt]	（動）想 （think的過去式）；認為
same [sem]	（形）相同的
rather [ˈræðɚ]	（副）相當
tan [tæn]	（名）棕褐色
make-up [ˈmekˌʌp]	（名）化妝品
match [mætʃ]	（動）相配
choose [tʃuz]	（動）選擇

37. had better
最好

I think you'd better tell Jenny...

文法句型解說

had better

had better是「最好～」的意思，如果你要勸對方「最好
是這麼做」，如你知道對方快遲到了，你就跟他說：
You had better leave now, or you'll be late.
你最好現在走，否則你會遲到。
had better這個片語如果是用在「I had better...」這個句
型，則是在說「自己最好這麼做」，例如：你知道約翰
在等你的電話，所以你要說「我最好打個電話給他」，
免得他等得不耐煩，你可以說 I had better give John a
call.

●提醒別人最好怎麼做的說法。

[M] Mary, let's get going and have this project done real fast.

I promised Jenny I'd take her out for a soda as soon as we're finished.

[W] I think you'd better tell Jenny that you'll be busy all afternoon.

[M] But you said we'd be finished in no time.

[W] That was before I knew we'd have to redesign our layout.

[M] 瑪麗，繼續做吧，盡快把這個企畫做完。
我答應珍妮，等我們做完就帶她去喝汽水。

[W] 我想你最好告訴珍妮，你整個下午都會很忙。

[M] 但是，你說我們快做完了。

[W] 那是在我知道我們必須重新設計版面之前說的。

Tip !---英語小知識

get going

get going的意思是「去做某件事情」，當大家休息了一陣子之後，你要大家繼續做時，你就可以催促大家說We need to get going.，你也可以說 Let's get going and have it done.（我們大家繼續做，把它做完。）

We need to get going. 也可以用在你去參加一個宴會要離開時說的，這個時候 We need to get going. 的意思就是「我們該走了。」

或是，你們要去某個地方，你說 Let's get going.，意思就是「我們走吧。」

soda

一般汽水總稱 soda，若要問對方要不要喝汽水，你可以這樣說：Would you like a soda? 如果你有特定的飲料，如：7-Up（七喜）、Sprite（雪碧）、Coke（可口可樂）、Pepsi（百事可樂）或是橘子汁等，你要問對方要不要某樣你有的飲料，如你問對方要不要喝可樂，英語的說法是 Would you like some Coke?

be finished

be finished 的意思是「完成」，也可以說 be done，當你要說「我們事情做完了」，英語可以說 We're finished. 或是 We're done.

be finished也可以特別指出是某一件事情做完了，句型是「be finished with 某件事情」，如你問對方「功課做完了嗎？」，英語的說法是 Are you finished with your homework?

快熟句型---記住真好用

- ## Would you like a soda?
  你要不要喝汽水？

- I'm taking Mary out for a soda.
  我要帶瑪麗去冰店。

- You had better leave now.
  你最好現在就走。

- We need to get going.
  我們需要繼續做。

- Let me finish this real fast.
  讓我很快地把這個做完。

- Are you finished with your homework?
  你功課做完了嗎？

超實用單字---1秒就記住

project [ˈprɑdʒɛkt]	（名）專案；企畫
fast [fæst]	（形）快
promise [ˈprɑmɪs]	（動）保證；答應
soda [ˈsodə]	（名）汽水
finish [ˈfɪnɪʃ]	（動）完成
busy [ˈbɪzɪ]	（形）忙的
redesign [ˌridɪˈzaɪn]	（動）重新設計

layout	['le,aʊt]	（名）版面設計
plenty	['plɛntɪ]	（名）很多
homework	['hom,wɝk]	（名）家庭作業

I'm on the phone.

文法句型解說

phone

phone 這個字當動詞，是「打電話給某人」的意思，要說「打電話給某人」，英語可以說 phone 某人，或是 phone up 某人。

on the phone

「在講電話」，英語的說法是 on the phone。如果你在講電話，但是電視機的聲音太大了，你要說「把電視關小聲一點，我在講電話」，英語的說法就是 Turn down the TV. I'm on the phone.

如果你去接聽電話，對方說她叫瑪麗，想要跟約翰講電話，於是你去叫約翰，跟他說「有個叫做瑪麗的，要跟

你講電話」，英語的說法就是 There's a Mary on the phone for you.

或是你先生講完電話掛斷後，你問他說「剛剛電話中是誰」，英語的說法就是 Who was that on the phone?

answer the phone

「接聽電話」的英語是 answer the phone。若是電話鈴響了，你叫瑪麗去接聽電話，整句英語的說法是 Mary, could you answer the phone, please?

當電話鈴響時，你說「我去接電話好嗎」，或是「要我去接電話嗎」，英語的說法就是 Shall I answer the phone?

電話鈴響時，若是你要去接聽電話，也可以說：

I'll get it.

我去接。

說得漂亮--實況會話

●正在電話中，怎麼說？

W　Dad, can you help me with this?

M　Just a second, sweetheart.

W　Please Dad.

　　I need your help.

M　Wait just a second, honey.

　　I'm on the phone.

W 爸,你可以幫我忙嗎?

M 小甜心,稍等一下。

W 爸爸,拜託啦。
　我需要你幫忙。

M 小甜心,稍等一下。
　我在講電話。

●要去接電話的說法。

W Could you answer the phone, please?

Tell whoever it is I'm really busy.

M Sure. Where is it?

W In the hallway by the stairs.

M Okay, I'll get it.

I'll just take a message for you and you can call them back later.

W 請你接個電話。
不管是誰,跟他説,我真的很忙。

M 好,電話在哪裡?

W 在樓梯旁的走道那兒。

M 好的,我去接電話。
我就請他們留話,你再回他們電話。

快熟句型---記住真好用

- Jenny invited me over to her home for dinner tonight.

珍妮邀請我今晚去她家吃晚飯。

over

over 當副詞時，可以接在動詞的後面，表示「從某個地方到另一個地方」的意思，如你說「瑪麗邀請我過去她家」，英語的說法是 Mary invited me over to her home.

又如你說你今早看到約翰，你走過去跟他打招呼，但是他沒認出你，英語的說法就是 I went over to say hello but he didn't recognize me.

快熟句型---記住真好用

- Has Mary phoned yet?
  瑪麗有沒有打電話來？

- You'd better phone John and tell him we'll be late.
  你最好打電話給約翰，跟他說我們會晚一點。

- I bet they'll phone up with some excuses.
  我打賭他們會打電話來給我們一些藉口。

- I'll be at home tonight waiting for your call.
  我今晚會在家等你的電話。

- There's a Mary on the phone for you.
  有個叫瑪麗的，打電話要找你。

- Could you answer the phone please?
  請你去聽電話好嗎？

- Shall I answer the phone?
  我去聽電話好嗎？

超實用單字---1秒就記住

second ['sɛkənd]	（名）片刻
phone [fon]	（名）電話（動）打電話
answer ['ænsɚ]	（動）回答
really ['rilɪ]	（動）真的
busy ['bɪzɪ]	（形）忙的
hallway ['hɔl,we]	（名）走道
stairs [stɛrz]	（名）樓梯
message ['mɛsɪdʒ]	（名）留言
wore [wor]	（動）穿；戴（wear的過去式）
invite [ɪn'vaɪt]	（動）邀請
bet [bɛt]	（動）打賭
excuse [ɪks'kjus]	（名）藉口

39. The phone is ringing.
電話鈴響了。

Here's a list of all the callers.

文法句型解說

ring

ring 是「鈴響」的意思,「門鈴響了」或是「電話鈴響了」,都是用 ring 這個字,例如:「電話在響,誰有空去接電話」,英語的說法是,

The phone is ringing.

Could someone answer the phone?

ring 也可以當動詞,是「按門鈴」的意思,例如:你跟弟弟到了外婆家,你跟弟弟說「去按門鈴」,這句話英語的說法就是 Go ring the doorbell。你弟弟去按了門鈴,但是沒有人來應門,他就回來跟你說,

I rang the doorbell, but no one came.

我按了門鈴,但是沒有人來應門。

ring 也可以做「打電話」的意思,例如:你昨天打電

話給瑪麗，但是她不在，你今天遇到她，你就可以跟她說，

I rang you yesterday, but you weren't in.
我昨天打電話給你，但是你不在。

說得漂亮--實況會話

●電話響不停，怎麼說？

M Hi, I'm home.

W Good. The phone hasn't stopped ringing for you all day.

M Did Mary call?

W I don't know.

Here's a list of all the callers.

You can find out for yourself.

M 嗨，我回來了。
W 很好，找你的電話一整天響個不停。

M 瑪麗有沒有打電話來？
W 我不知道。
這是打電話找你的人的名單。
你自己去看。

●按門鈴，要這麼說。

M I don't think they're home.

W Did you try ringing the doorbell?

M | I rang the doorbell, but no one came.

W | Okay then, come on.

We'll just try back later.

M 我想他們並不在家。

W 你有沒有按門鈴看看？

M 我按了，但是沒有人來應門。

W 那，走吧。
我們有空再來。

Tip !---英語小知識

try

當你想得到某些結果時，你可能需要試試一些方法看看，英語的説法是「try +動名詞」，這裡的動名詞（動詞 + ing）是「你試著去做的這個動詞的動名詞」，例如你跟弟弟到外婆家，你叫弟弟去叫門，他回來跟你説外婆可能不在，你問他説「你有沒有按門鈴看看」，按門鈴的英語是 ring the doorbell，因為你要把「ring the doorbell」放在 try 的後面，所以 ring 要改成動名詞「ringing」，英語的説法就是 Did you try ringing the doorbell?

快熟句型---記住真好用

- I rang you yesterday but you weren't in.
  我昨天打電話給你，但是你不在。

- The phone hasn't stopped ringing all day.
  一整天電話響個不停。

- I rang the doorbell but no one came.
  我按了門鈴，但是沒有人來。

ring [rɪŋ]	（動）鈴響；按門鈴
list [lɪst]	（名）名單
caller [ˈkɔlɚ]	（名）打電話者
try [traɪ]	（動）嘗試
doorbell [ˈdorˌbɛl]	（名）門鈴
rang [ræŋ]	（動）鈴響；按門鈴（ring的過去式）
stopped [stɑpt]	（動）停止（stop的過去分詞）

40. keep company
作伴

Where are you going?

文法句型解說

keep 某人 company

company 這個字一般學過的意思是「公司」，它還另一個常見的用法就是「作伴」的意思。如果某人獨自一個人在家，你說我要去跟他作伴，英語的說法就是 keep 某人 company，例如：瑪麗她先生出差去了，你說我要去她家跟她作伴，英語的說法是 I'm going over to Mary's to keep her company.

have company

company 這個字也可以做「客人」的意思。例如你看到隔壁史密斯家門口停了四部車子，你要說「隔壁史密斯家好像有客人」，英語的說法是 It looks like the Smiths have company.

expect company

company 當「客人」的意思，也常用在說「我們有客人要來」，英語的說法是 We're expecting company.

說得漂亮--實況會話

●和別人作伴，這麼說。

[M] Where are you going?

[W] I'm going over to Mary's to keep her company.

[M] That's nice of you.

I hope she feels better soon.

[W] I'll tell her you said so.

See you later.

[M] 你要去哪裡？

[W] 我要去瑪麗家，跟她作伴。

[M] 你真好。

我希望她很快能好一點。

[W] 我會把你的話，跟她說。

再見。

●有客人要來，可以這麼說。

W Do you want to go out for a drink after work?

M I'd love to but I can't.
We're expecting company.

W Really?

M Yes, my wife's relatives are coming for the weekend.

W 下班後，要不要一起去喝一杯？
M 我是想去，但是我不能去。
我們有客人要來。

W 真的？
M 是的，我太太的親戚要來度週末。

Tip !---英語小知識

expect company

有客人要來的說法是 expect company，如會話中的句子：We're expecting company. 如果是指「家裡來了客人」，英文的用法是 have company，例如：

It looks like the Smiths have company.
史密斯家好像有客人。

- I'm going over to Mary's to keep her company.
  我要去瑪麗家，跟她作伴。

- I'll stay to keep you company.
  我會留下來，跟你作伴。

- We are expecting company this evening.
  我們今晚有客人。

- It looks like the Smiths have company --- there are four cars in front of their house.
  史密斯家好像有客人，他們家門前有四部車子。

超實用單字---1秒就記住

expect [ɪk'spɛkt]	（動）預期；期待
company ['kʌmpənɪ]	（名）朋友；夥伴；作伴；客人
keep company	跟某人作伴
hope [hop]	（動）希望
feel [fil]	（動）感覺
soon [sun]	（副）很快地
relative ['rɛlətɪv]	（名）親戚
visit ['vɪzɪt]	（動）訪問；拜訪
stay [ste]	（動）停留

Part 2

用最簡單的英語
和外國人做生意

- It's very nice meeting you. 很高興與您會面。

- I will take your card. 讓我拿一張您的名片。

- Here is my card. 這是我的名片。

- We have a lot in common. 我們彼此有很多共同之處。

- How have you been? 您這一向可好嗎？

- Just let me know, if you need anything.
  有什麼需要的話，請儘管告訴我。

- I believe we have met before. 我相信我們曾經見過面。

- I remember that. 我記得那回事。

- You are quite good. 您非常的棒。

- You were not bad yourself. 您自己也不錯啊。

- What can I help you with? 我能幫您什麼忙嗎？

- You look familiar. 您看起來很面熟。

- You do too! 您也是！

- I have heard a lot about it. 關於這個東西，我聽了很多。

- It's simply amazing. 那實在不可思議。

- Let me set up the demonstration. 讓我把這個展示設立起來。

- I like that. 我喜歡那樣。

- I think I might pass. 我想我不要了。

- Thank you anyway. 還是很謝謝您。

- Allow me to show you.　請容許我展示給您看。

- That's a good idea.　那是個好主意。

- How about yours?　那您自己的呢？

- In that case, ~　那樣子的話，～

- Is the price negotiable?　價錢可以商量嗎？

- The price is too high.　價格太高了。

- Just try us.　請試用我們的產品吧。

- Take the big picture into account.　從大局來看。

- Our package is a better value.　我們的整套產品比較有價值。

- Our prices are lower.　我們的價錢比較低。

- I will get you those tomorrow.　我明天把那些東西給您拿來。

- When would be a good time?　幾時比較恰當？

- You get a lot more than what you expected.
  您得到的比您期許的還要多的多。

- Yes, we can.　是的，我們辦得到。

- I am hoping to speak with you.　我很希望跟您談談。

- Is he available?　他現在有空嗎？

- Great!　太好了！

- May I ask what this is regarding?　我能問您什麼事嗎？

- I wanted to introduce our new prices.
  我要介紹我們的新價目。

- How are you?　您好嗎？

- It's been a long time.　很久不見了。

- It's why I came to see you.　那就是我來見您的理由。

- Congratulations.　恭喜。

- It won't take long.　不會擔誤太久的。

- Do you remember me?　您還記得我嗎？

- Thank you for your time.　謝謝您撥冗。

- Our service is the best.　我們的服務是最好的。

- We handle everything for you.　我們幫您處理所有的事情。

- I understand.　我瞭解。

- Imagine how much of your time will be saved.
  想想看，可以節省您多少時間。

- I promise.　我答應。

- Just leave it all to me.　把所有的事都留給我辦吧。

- I'm glad to hear it.　聽到這件事，我很高興。

- Let me explain.　讓我來跟您解釋。

- We have an automated system.　我們有一套自動化系統。

- You make the choice.　您來做選擇。

- Sounds good. 聽起來很好。

- What's next? 下一步是什麼？

- I like it. 我喜歡這個主意。

- It will save you time and money. 可以節省您的時間和金錢。

- What happens if ~? 如果～會怎樣？

- Your satisfaction is guaranteed. 我們包君滿意。

- There are no time restrictions. 沒有時間限制。

- No problem. 毫無問題。

- I can't believe that. 真叫我難以置信。

- We have an excellent policy. 我們有一套很好的策略做法。

- You may get an exchange. 您可以換貨。

- That would be a great choice for you.
  那對您而言是很好的選擇。

- Let me point out a few other things.
  讓我把其他幾樣東西挑出來給您看。

- They might be just what you are looking for.
  他們可能就是您在找的貨色。

- I am here to help you out. 我在這裡上班，就是要幫您忙的。

- All at the same low price. 所有的訂價都是一樣低。

- Save time. 您可以節省時間。

- Call us and we will be there.
  請給我們一通電話，我們就會出現。

- Let me see them.　讓我看看那些東西。

- The selection here is huge.　這裡可供選擇的樣式很多。

- This could be your only chance.　這可能是您唯一的機會。

- Why do you say that?　您為什麼這麼說？

- Don't take chances.　請千萬別冒險。

- I see.　我明白了。

- Bring your husband by.　請把您的丈夫帶來。

- Your order will be delivered soon.　您訂的貨很快就會送去。

- We accept credit cards.　我們收信用卡。

- We will match any deal.　我們可以比照別人的價錢。

- Thank you so much for having me.　非常謝謝您邀請我來。

- You will love our products.　您會喜歡我們的產品的。

- Watch our demonstration.　請注意看我們的展示。

- You will be convinced.　您會信服的。

- This would be a great buy.　這將會是一個很划算的交易。

- Let me tell you about our service.
  請容許我告訴您我們的服務。

- It offers more options than the others.
  它比其他的提供更多的選擇。

- We need to discuss price.　我們需要談談價錢。

- The prices are customized.　價格依顧客不同需求而定。

- What do you mean by that?　您說這話是什麼意思？

- I am sure you will be totally satisfied with us.
  我肯定您對我們會感到完全滿意。

- I will call you tomorrow.　我明天會打個電話給您。

- It's worth it.　那是值得的。

- Really?　真的嗎？

- I hope you understand.　我希望您能瞭解。

- Thank you for your time.　謝謝您撥空到這裡來。

- I'll call you in a month.　我一個月後，再打電話給您。

- By then our prices may be lower.
  屆時，我們的價目也許會降低。

- Here is my card.　讓我給您我的名片。

- I am sorry.　很抱歉。

- May I ask why?　可以問為什麼嗎？

- Absolutely.　當然了。

- We can decrease your monthly payment.
  我們可以降低您每一個月的付款額。

- Let me call my supervisor.　我來跟我的主管打個電話。

- I am willing to come down a little.
  我很願意把價格降低一點點。

- That's fine.　那樣很好。

- I appreciate it.　我很感激。

- It wouldn't take that much time or money to do it.
  要做的話，不會花很多的時間和金錢。

- Let me explain again.　請容我再跟您解釋一下。

- Anyone can use this system.　每個人都會用這一套系統。

- All right.　好吧。

- Let me think it over.　讓我再考慮考慮。

- Allow me.　請讓我來。

- You'll see what time and money we can save you.
  您會發現我們可以幫您節省多少時間和金錢。

- Can we set an appointment now?
  我們現在可以訂個約會了嗎？

- I can meet with you after lunch.　我午餐後，可以與您會面。

- It's not difficult to use.　使用上沒有困難。

- You never know.　會發生什麼事，您也不知道。

- May I help you?　我能為您效勞嗎？

- What did you need?　您需要什麼東西呢？

- When is a good time for us to meet?
  我們幾時會面，會比較恰當呢？

- See you then.　到時候見。

- That would be fine.　那樣還可以。

- Do you have some free time?　您有沒有空？

- Call before you come.　您來之前，請打個電話。

- Glad to see you.　很高興看到您。

- No worse than usual.　不會比平常差。

- That works for me.　那樣對我而言，行得通。

- I have got a solution to your problem.
  對於您的問題，我有解決方法。

- How does that sound so far?　到目前為止，聽起來如何？

- I'll wait here.　我要在這裡等。

- I look forward to seeing you again.　我熱切盼望再與您會面。

- We sell these by the box.　我們是一箱一箱的賣。

- That's out of my price range.　那已經超出我們的出價範圍。

- I'll make you a deal.　我來幫您弄個好價錢。

- If you buy today, you buy one get one free.
  您如果今天購買的話，買一送一。

- How much do you charge?　您要價多少？

- It will be nice to connect a name with a face.
  能耳聞大名之後再親自見面真好。

- It's very easy to find.　很容易就可以找到。

- Is that all right?　這樣可以嗎？

- Here she is.　她來了。

- I appreciate it.　我很感激。

- Call us if you have questions.
如果您有問題的話，請打電話給我們。

- I'll be right over.　我馬上就過來。

- Where are you?　您在哪裏？

- I am calling from my car phone.　我從我的汽車電話打電話。

- I was caught in it.　我被卡住了。

- It's hard to get around.　很不容易避開。

- Who is this?　請問是誰？

- I am running a little late.　我會比較遲一點。

- Please excuse my lateness.　請原諒我的遲到。

- I'll be there as soon as I can.　我會儘快趕到。

- Our price is considerably lower.
我們的價格，比較之下，相當的低。

- Your needs determine the charges.　您的需求決定價格。

- I can buy for you for 5% commission.
我可以幫您採買，佣金只要 5%。

- We will bill you later.　我們稍後再給您寄帳單。

- Explain to me.　請跟我解釋一下。

- Tell me what you need. 告訴我您需要的是什麼。

- There is no extra charge for that. 就算那樣，不另外加價。

- May I help you find something?
  您要買什麼東西，可以幫您找嗎？

- I'll take a look. 讓我看看。

- What are your priorities? 您的首要條件是什麼？

- I think you'll really like this one.
  我認為您真的會喜歡這個東西。

- I will be happy to. 我很樂意這樣做。

- Thank you for your help. 很感謝您的幫助。

- No, thanks. 不用，謝謝。

- I remember you. 我記得您。

- That's right. 一點都不錯。

- What model is it? 那是哪一種機型？

- How low are you talking? 您所說的價格是多低？

- I can't wait to see it. 我等不及要看一看。

- You can return the product within 7 days.
  七天之內，您可以把貨退回來。

- Let me see what I have. 讓我看看我有什麼貨。

- How about this one? 這一件怎麼樣？

- That's great. 那樣很好。

- Your orders will be handled by the most experienced employee.
  您訂的貨將由最有經驗的員工來處理。

- I don't see a problem with that. 我看沒什麼問題。

- We can set it up for you. 我們可以幫您設立起來。

- I'm just kidding. 我只是開玩笑。

- You have been very kind. 您的人很親切。

- Sure, no problem. 當然，沒有問題。

- It's a protection of your benefit. 這是保障您的利益。

- You receive a better price by paying it off now.
  一次付清的話，價格上比較好一點。

- We take cash and traveler's checks only.
  我們只收現金和旅行支票。

- Do you have an ID? 您有沒有身分證件？

- I will be willing to work with you on payment.
  關於付款方式，我很願意跟您商量出一個辦法。

- I can't do it. 我辦不到。

- I'm willing to negotiate. 我很願意做商量。

- Make me an offer. 出個價錢吧。

- How about meeting right in the middle?
  在價格上您加一半，我退一半怎麼樣？

- That is the lowest price I can offer. 那是我能賣的最低價了。

- Believe me. 請相信我。

- I think we could work something out.
  我想我們一定可以商量出什麼辦法來的。

- I would give you a discount. 我可以給您打折。

- Somewhere in the neighborhood of 2,000 dollars.
  大約在 2,000 元左右。

- I can live with that. 對我來説還可以。

- What do you think? 您意下如何？

- We are a little high on price. 我們的價格是高了一點。

- I see. 我明白了。

- We can't cut our prices any more. 我們的價格不能再降了。

- I am willing to drop the price a little. 我願意把價格降一點。

- It's nowhere near what you are offering.
  那與您所出的價錢差太遠了。

- You're very welcome. 您不用客氣。

- I will see you later. 再見了。

- I can do nothing more. 我已盡力了。

- We have a deal. 我們達成了一個交易。

- Accidents happen. 意外總會發生的。

- Nothing will break. 所有東西都不會出錯。

- You won't regret. 您不會後悔的。

- Good news for you.　告訴您一個好消息。

- I know you won't be disappointed.　我知道您不會失望的。

- What is the reason for your hesitation?
  是什麼原因讓您猶豫不決呢？

- We can lower the payment for you.
  我們可以把您的付款額降低一點。

- That's correct.　一點都沒錯。

- It's not I who charge you that.　並不是我收您這些錢。

- It's standard.　那是標準收費。

- That is a standard charge.　那是標準收費。

- Sounds great.　聽起來很好。

- We are in no hurry.　我們一點都不急。

- I don't have a problem with that.
  在我這個方面，沒有什麼問題。

- I'll make you a copy.　我複印一份給您。

- We should take a step back.　我們應該後退一步，不要插手。

- I am not sure.　我不是很確定。

- I will hope so.　但願如此。

- I don't see any problems.　我看不出有什麼問題。

- I don't see any problems with the contract.
  這一張合約，我看不出有什麼問題。

- Does your side have any more questions?
  貴方還有其他問題嗎？

- We are bound by law.　我們是受法律約束的。

- Are you ready to sign?　你們現在可以簽了嗎？

- We have a witness.　我們有見證人。

- Let's put it in writing.　我們白紙黑字寫下來吧！

- Good idea.　好主意。

- You are just fine.　您自己就可以了。

- Just sign the contract.　請簽這一張合同。

- I will just wait.　我就在這裡等。

- That's fine.　沒有問題。

- That's all right.　沒有關係。

- Sign the contract first.　請先簽這一張合約。

- You won't cancel.　您不會取消合約的。

- We will think about it.　我們會考慮考慮。

- What do you mean?　您是什麼意思？

- That's understandable.　那是可以理解的。

- What time?　幾時？

- I'll do that.　我會這樣做。

- Will you do me a favor?　您能幫我一個忙嗎？

- Is that you?　是您嗎？

- I can't believe it.　我簡直不敢相信。

- What are you up to?　您近來如何？

- Would you care to join us?　要不要加入我們？

- Nice to meet you.　很高興與您會面。

- I would love to do that.　我很高興能這樣做。

- I'll be there.　我會參加的。

- The sooner the better.　越快越好。

- How are you?　您好嗎？

- I need it.　我真的需要。

- I know the feeling.　我體會得出這種感覺。

- I love New York.　我喜歡紐約。

- Everything was all right.　每一件事都很好。

- It's been a long day.　今天工作好多。

- I was a little concerned.　我有一些擔心。

- Don't worry.　不要擔心。

- It was a long flight.　此趟飛行很久。

- Let's go.　我們走吧。

- I will help you with your luggage.　讓我幫您提行李。

- Let's go and have some fun.　走吧，我們找樂子去。

- The hotel tab has been taken care of.
  旅館帳單已經幫您付了。

- You tell me. 您把您的意思說出來吧。

- Do you play? 您玩嗎？

- All right. 好吧。

- Don't worry about dressing up. 不用為正式穿著而操心。

- There's a good idea. 那是個好主意。

- Are you sure? 您確定嗎？

- Let's have a good time. 讓我們盡情的玩吧。

- It's on me. 我請客。

- I prefer soft music. 我喜歡聽輕音樂。

- Do you work out regularly? 您經常做運動嗎？

- Let's play sometime. 我們找個時間玩玩吧。

- I'll take it easy on you. 我會讓您的。

- Deal. 一言為定。

- We tee off at 8:00. （高爾夫球）我們八點鐘開打。

- That was nothing. 小意思沒有什麼。

- It meant a lot to me. 對我來說意義重大。

- You are very thoughtful. 您很體貼。

- When is your birthday? 您的生日是什麼時候？

- Guess what I got.　您猜我得到什麼？

- I need the address.　我需要您的住址。

- Congratulations.　恭喜。

- What do you prefer?　您比較喜歡什麼？

- You don't have to do that.　您可以不必如此的。

- It's not for business.　這並不是為了生意上的往來。

- You can't refuse that.　您千萬不能拒絕。

- I am glad about your new job.　我為您的新職位感到高興。

- I hate to see you leave.　我很不願意看到您離開。

- We did good.　我們合作愉快。

- I enjoyed working with you.　與您一道工作，非常愉快。

- I'm feeling pretty good.　我覺得精神舒爽。

- That's good to hear.　很高興聽到這樣的消息。

- Get well soon.　祝您早日痊癒。

- You really deserved it.　您是實至名歸，應得的。

- Can I do anything to help?
  我可以為您做一點事，幫一點忙嗎？

- I am really glad to help.　我是很樂意幫忙的。

- Thank you so much.　非常感謝您。

- I want to say thanks again.　我要再度向您道謝。

- You sound great.　您聽起來非常好。

- Good.　太好了。

- You are really a salesman.　您真不愧是個推銷員。

- Let's continue to do business together.
  讓我們繼續在商務上合作吧。

- I am sure I can convince you.　我很確定我可以説服您的。

- They are pretty good in quality.　那些東西品質非常好。

- They are of great value.　那些東西很有價值。

- You will find they are very helpful.　您會發現他們很有價值。

- That service is free.　那項服務是免費的。

- You receive a discount by ordering today.
  今天下訂單的話有折扣。

- When did you order it?　您是什麼時候訂貨的？

- Let me check on that for you.　讓我幫您查。

- Let me look that up.　讓我幫您查一下。

- It is back-ordered.　目前缺貨。

- We will send it to you at no extra cost.
  我們會另外寄給您，不收錢。

- Do you have the tracking number?　您有沒有查尋號碼？

- Please hold one moment.　請暫時不要掛電話。

- I'm sorry.　很抱歉。

- We will send out another one. 我們會另外再寄一份。

- Thank you for your patience. 很感謝您這樣有耐心。

- It's in the mail. 我們已經寄出去了。

- I know what happened. 我知道發生什麼事了。

- What happened? 發生什麼事呢？

- Thank you for informing me. 謝謝您通知我。

- I'll get on this right away. 我馬上會處理這件事。

- You know how the mail is. 您也知道郵寄是什麼情況的。

- Good deal. 太好了。

- They are 90 days past due. 他們已經過期九十天了。

- That is the next step. 那是我們的下一步。

- It will appear on your credit record.
  這件事會在你們的信用報告顯示出來。

- We don't want to penalize you. 我們很不願意懲罰你們。

- You have been late on the payments.
  你們應付的款已經過期。

- That would be better. 那樣做比較好。

- Everything is great. 每件事都很好。

- We made a good decision. 我們下的決策非常正確。

- Do you have any more questions? 您有沒有其他的問題？

- Feel free.　請別客氣的提出來。

- I am here to help you.　我上班就是為您服務的。

- Thanks anyway.　無論如何還是謝謝您。

- We ran out yesterday.　我們昨天用光了。

- Is everything OK?　凡事都好嗎？

- How are things going with you?　一切如意嗎？

- I sure hope I can answer them for you.
  我真的希望我能夠幫您解答問題。

- It does appear that way.　看起來就是那個樣子。

- We will be expecting your call.　我們期待您給我們打電話。

- I am sorry that I can't help more.
  很對不起，不能再進一步幫忙了。

- We can't give you your money back.
  我們不能把您的錢退給您。

- I'll be over as soon as possible.　我會儘快趕過來。

- I will be right there.　我馬上過來。

- Is there a problem?　有問題嗎？

- I will be right over.　我馬上就過去。

- I'll have someone there.　我會請一個人過去。

- Whatever it is.　不管如何。

- Where are you located?　你們坐落在何處？

- We can repair the equipment on time.
  我們會及時把設備修理好。

- We will replace it. 我們會換一個新的給您。

- That's right. 一點都不錯。

- That's OK. 沒有問題。

- It will be close though. 會很接近截止日期喲。

- I will keep you posted. 我會隨時通知您。

- How long will it take for mail to get here from the USA?
  從美國寄信到這裡要多久？

- You are good at keeping in touch. 您對保持聯絡很在行。

- Here are the names and addresses.
  您要的名字和住址在這裡。

- What is the telephone number? 電話號碼是幾號？

- Why don't you try to call them?
  您為什麼不試試打電話給他們？

- I would appreciate that very much. 我會非常感激。

- Let me give you the information about it.
  我們把關於這件事的資料給您。

- Excuse me. 對不起。

- I am very interested. 我感到很有興趣。

- Where do I send the registration form?
  我應該把報名表寄到什麼地方？

- Please send it as soon as possible.　請儘快的寄過來。

- They cost more.　他們的費用比較高。

- It sounds good.　聽起來不錯。

- It's pretty crowded.　非常擁擠。

- That should work.　那應該行得通。

- Good point.　好論點！

- I will meet you there.　我會在那裡與您見面。

- How do I do that?　我應該怎麼做？

大膽說：流利英語的捷徑

英語系列：47

作者／張瑪麗
出版者／哈福企業有限公司
地址／新北市板橋區五權街16號
電話／(02) 2945-6285　傳真／(02) 2945-6986
郵政劃撥／31598840　戶名／哈福企業有限公司
出版日期／2018年4月
定價／NT$ 299元 (附MP3)

全球華文國際市場總代理／采舍國際有限公司
地址／新北市中和區中山路2段366巷10號3樓
電話／(02) 8245-8786　傳真／(02) 8245-8718
網址／www.silkbook.com　新絲路華文網

香港澳門總經銷／和平圖書有限公司
地址／香港柴灣嘉業街12號百樂門大廈17樓
電話／(852) 2804-6687　傳真／(852) 2804-6409
定價／港幣100元 (附MP3)

圖片／shuttlestock
email／haanet68@Gmail.com
網址／Haa-net.com
facebook／Haa-net 哈福網路商城

國家圖書館出版品預行編目資料

大膽說：流利英語的捷徑 / 張瑪麗著. --
新北市：哈福企業, 2018.04

　　面；　公分. -- (英語系列；47)

　ISBN 978-986-94966-9-8(平裝附光碟片)

1.英語 2.會話

805.188　　　　　　　　107003266